Before the Witches

Before the Witches

An Original Novella

Karina Cooper

AVONIMPULSE

EPub Edition June 2011 ISBN: 9780062105172

Print Edition July 2011 ISBN: 9780062115430

10 9 8 7 6 5 4 3 2 1

Chapter One

"What's her name?"

The voice came as if through a fog, each syllable laced with a leer so thick she could practically taste its acid on her tongue. Ekaterina Zhuvova blinked away the thick cotton of exhaustion filling her head, gaze focusing with some effort on the two men standing at the back of the small living room.

"Elena," Ivan said, nodding with almost paternal-like pride at the red-haired woman leaning back against the couch, her full breasts pushed up by her position. She raked a lascivious gaze over the stranger's tall body. "She is most experienced with making a man forget a few hours, eh?"

This man wasn't like the others Katya had seen come and go from this house before. He wasn't as tall as some she'd entertained, but he was clearly strong enough to hold his own and still a foot taller than her petite five feet and two inches. His shoulders were broad, chest tight with muscle beneath a navy blue cotton T-shirt and a button-downopen flannel shirt. Long legs encased in worn denim planted with near military precision, though his shaggy, slightly spiky black hair told her whatever his demeanor, he wasn't active duty. Ex-military? Private contractor?

A taste for foreign girls developed overseas and couldn't kick the habit? She knew *that* type, all right.

"Her?" The man's gaze settled on her, and Katya looked away. *Please, don't pick me.*

"Katya," Ivan said, and the warmth left his voice as he turned his head. She lowered her eyes before he could see her anger as his mouth worked, but he didn't spit. She knew he wanted to.

"No good?" the man asked, his tone lazily assessing.

"Ved'ma," Ivan explained with a shrug. She barely kept from wincing, schooling her features into calm.

"Is that her name?"

"No." Ivan eyed her. "She is strange one, even in my country."

"Strange." One eyebrow raised.

Ivan grinned. "She is knowing exactly what a man likes. This is both good thing and bad. I save her for the men who are less sure of self. She is very good with first-time, eh?"

She was beyond blushing, but the flush staining her cheeks now was anger. She ducked her head before she said something guaranteed to put her in lock-up.

Ivan was half-right. She'd always been good at reading people. She didn't know how or why, but she always knew when a person was lying. It wasn't the same as what Ivan was suggesting, but she'd gotten damn good at that, too.

Her talent wasn't the gift he made it out to be. It had made for a rocky childhood in St. Petersburg's destitute streets. Cast out by the neighborhood children, they'd hunted her into the desperate sanctuary of her mother's single-room flat. Their jeers still haunted her dreams.

Ved'ma, ved'ma! Ubyei yee!

She'd found no solace from the adults who felt threatened by a little girl with an uncanny grasp of deceit. It was no wonder she'd bartered everything she had, including her own body, to get to America.

In America, they didn't care about witches. That belief had proved true.

They were too busy paying for her physical prowess to care about any other talents, and the time they spent lying to her meant she got damned good at reading between the lines. She knew a lot. She knew what was truth and what was lie. She knew how to ask the right questions, and how to translate the half-truths and lies. Men spent a lot of time lying to themselves. Especially when screwing a strange girl in a dingy house.

Her gaze flicked back to meet the client's, and this time, she didn't look away.

His mouth tightened. "What about the one in the chair?"

Dismissed. Thank God. Katya angled her shoulder against the wall. If she sat, if she so much as perched on the end of the couch by Elena, she knew she'd fall asleep. She was beyond fatigued. Brutal nightmares had filled her dreams all night long, and she'd dragged herself out of bed this morning feeling as if she'd been awake for years.

Every time she closed her eyes last night, she'd dreamed of death. Fires, floods, scenes of wildly absurd apocalyptic chaos.

It was as if her brain had taken all of her plans and launched off into a thousand worst-case scenarios, each culminating in the ludicrously detailed destruction of the world. She woke up at least a dozen times, sweaty and shaking.

Now, it was all Katya could do to keep her eyelids open as a Russian pimp and a stranger discussed human beings like they were at some kind of flea market.

Tomorrow was the day. The day she and all the other immigrant girls trapped in this hellhole would be free. The day that all her plans would come to fruition. Almost everything had fallen into place, with the sole exception of the police aid she'd tried to ask for only this morning. They'd denied her. Refused to believe her.

She hated this country, sometimes. It would be different once she was free. Once they were *all* free. The girls knew what to do. They were ready.

Terrified, but ready. One more day.

And every hour closer made moments like *this* feel impossible to handle.

Another man. Another sweaty session on a stained mattress. Another lie batted through her lashes and strained through a smile she'd long since learned to cultivate. She didn't think she could do it.

"I want her."

She was sure she looked like hell warmed over, so even with Ivan's impatient gestures , it took her too long to realize that the mysterious man with the dark hair and five o'clock shadow had chosen her.

Katya straightened again, keenly aware of the client's assessing gaze as she approached the men. She didn't dare say anything. This was the bargaining moment, the time when only Ivan could speak. Business, he called it.

Human trafficking was definitely a business.

Ivan was a large man, more girth than height, but he was as hard and worn as brick and not given to patience. His thick jowls and caterpillar eyebrows gave him the appearance of a bull dog; a reputation equally as earned. He was their warden. Their money-handler, and their guard.

Only he didn't guard *them*. He guarded the men who paid to screw them.

And occasionally skimmed from the honey himself. He lowered his head and glared at her in silent warning.

Behave, or she'd live to regret it.

"You tell her what you like," he said, snagging Katya's arm. "She will do it. *Anything*." She bit her lip, swallowing a startled sound as the large Russian swung her around, then shoved her hard into the other man's chest.

Large, strong hands closed over her shoulders.

"She is hellcat," Ivan leered, one fleshy eye closing in a wink. "Good."

The only two other girls not already occupied watched with impassive faces as Ivan shook a finger under Katya's nose. "You be good girl for this one, eh?" he told her, his accent thick enough to serve borscht on.

Unlike hers , his accent was all natural.

Katya nodded, forcing her lips up into a wide, wicked smile. At the same time, she arched her back, forcing the curve of her backside into the stranger's groin.

His fingers tightened on her shoulders. "What's the cost?" the man asked.

Ivan arced a fleshy hand through the air. "This one, she is thousand more than negotiated," he said, and Katya's eyes widened.

A thousand American dollars *more?* Impossible. Ivan's boss didn't barter his girls for that much, at least not these girls in this ramshackle Renton brothel. Did the always absent Mikoyan know about this arrangement?

Who was this man that Ivan would demand more money? A politician? A new money launderer? Someone with a business angle that Ivan's boss wanted to squeeze for everything it was worth?

Dark brown eyes met hers briefly, then skated away. "Fine," he said tightly. "Jesus Christ."

"Of course, she is more expensive, but you want her. Next time," Ivan added as he gestured to the room, "maybe you try another."

"Right." The man nodded to the small backpack on the floor. "Mikoyan's cut is in there. Count it while I'm busy," he said flatly, and didn't bother with any more pleasantries. Shifting his grip on her arm, he hauled her bodily out of the cramped living room. There was barely enough room in there for a couch and a television, much less five more people.

Katya stumbled as he pulled her purposefully towards the stairs. Behind them, the sudden blare of the television flickered to life.

"You are *hurting* me!" she protested as he jerked her up the stairs and into a cramped room.

The door clicked quietly into place, leaving Katya locked insidewith nothing but a dirty mattress and the man who'd just purchased her for the hour.

He didn't pay any attention to her accented protest, his fingers hard on her biceps as he spun her in place. Her pale hair slid into her eyes as he seized both arms and tucked her tightly against the door.

His dark brown eyes met hers, his face so close she could smell remnants of his aftershave. Something like fresh sawdust and pine. His angular features were suntanned, darkened by a five o'clock shadow that looked more like it was getting on towards ten.

He looked intent. Focused. And he damn well needed to let her go. Adrenaline forced her blood to surge, wiping away all traces of exhaustion.

She twisted; he pinned her shoulders back against the door. "How good is your English?" he demanded.

Katya stared up at him. That was his reason for holding her? He wanted to *talk?*

Her gaze trailed to the neck of his T-shirt, to the tell-tale bulge under his left shoulder. A matte black edge peeking from the open flannel made her eyes widen. A gun?

A cop? She sucked in a breath.

Those long fingers dug into her flesh.

She snapped her gaze back to his, her heart pounding in her ears. "Is good," she managed, deliberately thickening the Russian accent that still colored her otherwise excellent English. Pulling her persona around her like a shroud, she let her body soften against his.

Watched his pupils dilate as the lush curve of her breasts pushed into his chest.

Cop or not, he was a man. And all men had an easy button.

One more day, she told herself. One more man.

"I am understanding English very well," she purred. The tension at her arms lessened. Deliberately, she drew her tongue across her full lower lip.

His gaze pinned there, a whole lot warmer than it had been a moment ago.

"Well enough for hearing what you are wanting," she added huskily. A muscle leapt in his jaw as she leaned forward, pressing her lips against his chin. "Well enough for obeying. You like me?" Her mouth brushed against his whiskered jaw. "You want me, you are asking just for me, *da?*" Her lips drifted lower, explored the cords tense at his neck.

At his collar, just above his T-shirt. His skin was warm.

Her stomach clenched. To her surprise, not all of it was fear. Or disgust.

He jerked as her tongue slid out to taste the hollow of his throat. Suddenly, his hands constricted again, pushed her back against the door. The panel shook.

His eyes were hard. "Who are you?"

"Katya." That wasn't a lie, and he'd heard it already.

"Your *real* name," he said tersely.

For a moment, she froze. Paralyzed by indecision. She could ask him if he was on the take; she'd know the truth the instant it left his lips. But if his answer was *no*, she'd be in a world of trouble. He'd haul her to Ivan and she'd be left trying to explain why she was asking questions of the clients.

Especially questions about police.

No, she couldn't ask. He'd bartered for an hour of her body. Good cops didn't do that.

She frowned. Pouted, really. "Why?" she demanded petulantly. "Katya is not pretty?"

"Now."

Fine. "Ekaterina Mikhailovna Zhuvova," she said, so smoothly that she watched him blink at the onslaught of blurred syllables.

"Where are you from, Ekaterina Mikhailovna Zhuvova?" His echoed accent was damn near close to perfect.

"Moscow," she lied. St. Petersburg, actually, but it was all the same to Americans.

"Why were you at the police station this morning?"

Katya's eyes widened. So he *was* a cop. And given how buddy-buddy she'd seen him get with Ivan, not the kind of cop she desperately needed.

Her mind racing, she watched the intensity, the suspicion, in the dirty cop's features and recognized them for what they were. He was grilling her. Why? Did he have reason to suspect her?

The ability to *hear* a lie wasn't going to help her deliver her own pack of them. Her heart slamming in her chest, she managed, "Station? You are police?" She tried to shrink back, but he hadn't let her go. She didn't have to fake the fear in her voice as she begged, "*Please,* do not arrest me. Do not hurt me!" She allowed herself to shake in his grip, watched with some satisfaction as his expression banked to sudden surprise.

Then fury. He was . . . offended?

"I'm not going to hurt *you,*" he growled. It resonated like honesty.

It didn't matter. "You are police," she cried, as if it explained everything.

"Yeah, but I'm not—Son of a bitch." He let her go.

She slid out from between his body and the door, but the

only place to go was deeper into the tiny room. Any farther, and she'd be on the stained mattress.

The signal he expected, but not the one she wanted to send.

She'd had enough of this filthy room to last a lifetime. The water-stained walls, single mattress, and bare, scuffed floor would be indelibly imprinted on her brain forever.

She just had to last one more day. Which meant playing by this cop's rules. She clasped her hands under chin. "You are here to arrest Katya?"

The cop grunted. Then, seamlessly switching gears—and again surprising the hell out of her—he said in passable Russian, "I am not going to hurt you, Katya. I just want to know why you were at the station." So the bastard knew her language.

And he was still telling the truth.

Katya's shoulders rounded. She dipped her chin, letting her hair slide over her face in a light golden curtain. "They picked me up," she lied, this time in the same language he almost didn't butcher. "They were asking me questions. I told them I was visiting my sister."

The cops had claimed they needed more evidence than just the word of an illegal immigrant like her. Now she knew why. A cop on the take.

Why wasn't she more surprised?

He watched her as if trying to read the truth on her eyes, and she met his gaze squarely. *Believe me,* she prayed. Seven girls counted on his gullibility.

Katya started as he crossed the small room. She backpedaled, her stomach twisting around an icy knot of anticipation. Her heel hit the edge of the mattress, and she jerked.

He caught her arms, but there was nothing restraining

about it this time. He steadied her gently. His brow furrowing in tacit concern, he said, "My name is Nigel Ferris." *Truth,* whispered the tiny signal in the back of her brain. "Did you tell them that you were a—"

He hesitated, and she barely kept from laughing outright. Was it possible? Did he have trouble shaping his mouth around the word "whore"?

A dirty cop with morals. Now she'd seen *everything.*

Forcing her features into a mask of terrified sincerity, she shook her head until her hair swung. "*Nyet!* I say nothing."

His face shuttered, and she slowly took in a deep breath. Did he believe her? If not, she could end up very dead, very quick. There'd been girls who vanished before.

Lies spoken about their whereabouts.

Distraction. She could do distraction.

She stepped into him. Closed the distance between them, slid her hands up his chest. A part of her mind fragmented at finding him hot to the touch, even through his T-shirt. His muscles leapt under her palms; his heart slammed against her hand.

He wasn't as unaffected by her as he wanted to be.

And rightfully so; her role demanded she dress the part. Her too-thin T-shirt was white, her bra sweetheart pink and clearly obvious beneath it. It left two inches of her waist bare, hugged tight by low-rise jeans.

She looked edible. Fresh.

She looked like every other Russian girl off the boat who had ever been forced into prostitution.

And she knew how to act the part.

Rising up on her tip-toes, she hooked her fingers into the

collar of his shirt and said in her accented English, "You will not hurt Katya?"

His jaw shifted. His body all but vibrated against hers. Most men would have had her on her back by now.

Was he shy?

She flicked her tongue against the column of his throat. He sucked in a breath. "Katya will not hurt you," she murmured. She nuzzled the skin behind his ear, and his head moved. A fraction of an inch. Reluctant as hell, but there.

"Katya will make you feel nice," she whispered, just before she sank her teeth into the sensitive skin of his earlobe.

The sound he made was guttural, leashed taut.

So he had the same button as all the other men after all. The same weakness that would buy her the time to figure out what to do with a dirty cop.

She smiled against his skin.

A smile that faded as he once more caught her shoulders, wrenching her away. His eyes blazed in stormy black and brown; a wild intensity that ratcheted tension through her as he stared into her own.

Her heart leapt into her throat. "I—"

"They'll know if I don't," he muttered hoarsely, but more as if he spoke to himself than to her. Without warning, he pulled her hard against him. Caught her face between his palms and tipped her face up with impatient fingers.

Katya gasped.

He covered the sound with his lips, pulled the air from her lungs on a low, angry noise that did nothing to dull the sudden heat flushing her chest. Her stomach, and lower.

His lips were warm, firm against hers. Demanding. He

didn't coax, he didn't wait; Katya had long since learned never to expect it. He tilted her face up, thumbs at the corners of her mouth, and swept his tongue inside to taste her.

Her breath shuddered. The sensation seemed to light a fire in him; he dragged his tongue across hers. Teased it, coaxed it to follow back into his own mouth. The world simmered around her, danced wildly as if caught in a heat wave.

His eyelashes were black, she realized. The skin across his high cheekbones was taut, flushed with control and arousal and his body against hers was rock solid and—*Oh, God.*

For one moment, Katya forgot about her situation. She forgot about the other girls she was so desperately trying to protect; forgot about their jailer somewhere in the small house.

She forgot about the plans to escape this hellhole and the police who had turned her away.

There was only Nigel Ferris; dirty cop with a mouth to die for.

She closed her eyes. His hands left her face and she fisted her fingers in his shirt, hauling him closer. Begging him wordlessly to continue feasting from her lips. Tasting her soul. He groaned again. His arms came around her, dragged her off the floor. Wild, wanton, she wrapped her legs around his hips and tangled her fingers into his short, wavy hair.

He sank his teeth into her lower lip and she arched. The thick length of his erection ground against the front of her jeans and her skin caught fire. Gasping for breath, she could only moan helplessly as he held her as easily as if she were made of feathers, ground himself against her, devoured her identity and her willpower with a bruising kiss that would be sure to leave her lips swollen when he was done.

Arousal filled her so hard, so shockingly hot and fast, that she reeled.

It had been too long.

Why? Why a cop? A bad cop, even?

And then his hand crept under her shirt and she forgot that, too. Her world was suddenly comprised of the feel of his callused palm against her naked waist. Her ribs. And then hard and warm over the soft pink cup of her bra. She thrust herself into his hand, her fingers tight at the back of his neck.

"Not a good idea," he groaned against her mouth, each syllable a throaty curse. "Wait, stop, I—The hell!" He staggered, jarring Katya out of her reverie as somewhere beyond that door, girls screamed.

Her eyes snapped open.

"Shit!" Nigel dropped to his knees, still cradling Katya against his chest. "Get down!" He dropped her, and arousal flipped over to utter confusion, total fear. A raid! Were they being shot at? Was that—

"The floor," she gasped, struggling to push herself to her hands and knees. "It's moving!"

He didn't say anything, flattening a hand on her back. Katya grunted gracelessly as he pushed her to her stomach, and yelped as he covered her body with his. She felt dwarfed. Smothered.

Sick to her stomach.

He pushed her head down, folded his arms over her. The house shook and trembled around them. Plaster cracked, dingy white dust sifting to the floor as it rolled. Her stomach pitched and yawned; one ear plugged abruptly, and vertigo slammed into every nerve still trying to find mental footing.

Through the vee between his protective arm and the floor, she watched the mattress shimmy and vibrate its way to the other wall. Plaster fell in clumps, and she felt him tense over her. Heard him grit out something hard and painful.

He was protecting her. The dirty cop, the man who'd bargained with a Russian pimp for an hour of sex, was protecting her.

Katya's hands fisted as the room shuddered.

Who the hell was this man?

And why did she suddenly feel that she'd seen this earthquake coming?

Chapter Two

Detective Nigel Ferris shot out of that filthy little house like a bat out of hell. The brothel warden unlocked the bolts only reluctantly after he explained impatiently that the station would know if he didn't respond after an earthquake like that.

An earthquake, for God's sake. Talk about a sign from God.

The big Slavic muscle, Ivan—though Nigel would eat his badge if that was actually his name—had kept the money.

Nigel wrote it off. He was a man on a mission.

He rarely wasn't, but this time, as he navigated the busier-than-usual traffic of Seattle's midnight streets, his mission felt personal. It wasn't, of course, but damn it, it sure as shit felt like it was.

Ekaterina Mikhailovna Zhuvova. A mouthful even on a good day, and today wasn't a Goddamned good day. He'd done what he had to in order to put Ivan at ease. Hauled the petite blonde into that cramped room with its thin mattress and steeled himself to screw her and get out.

Ivan would have known if he didn't. Maybe there were cameras. Maybe the prostitute would have told her pimp the dirty cop hadn't done anything but ask her questions.

Nigel had expected to hate every second.

He didn't expect to lose himself in her mouth. To stare into her wide, summer blue eyes and feel the wrenching need to see those eyes cloud with lust. For him.

Shit. Him and God only knew how many other men before him. That earthquake had saved his ass.

Even as he'd hated to leave her. Leave them. Every drop of his blue-as-the-uniform blood sizzled at the necessity. He wanted to bust in, kick Ivan's ass and free the girls held captive, but he couldn't yet.

Not until he got to the bastard at the top of the prostitution ring. Nigel was looking forward to burying Mikoyan for life.

Maybe, just maybe, it'd make up for leaving those women behind.

The cell phone in his hand buzzed loudly as the unit tried to connect to busy landlines.

Nigel wrapped both hands around the wheel of his black SUV and cursed as the device in his ear chirped, "Seattle Police Department, hold."

The line clicked to static-filled classical music, and he swore as he disconnected. He wanted answers. Who was Ekaterina Zhuvova? Why had she *really* been at the station, and why the *fuck* hadn't he been told? This was his case. His.

A horn blared, and he wrenched his attention to the streets. That earthquake had taken them all by surprise. As far as he could see, the worst of the damage was a dark traffic light and the occasional debris scattered about already debris-clogged streets. Much like the plaster fragments that had rained down in that dingy, cramped room.

His nerves still recalled the feel of Katya's curves beneath him.

His brain still painted the terror in her eyes.

"Damn it," he muttered, downshifting as traffic slowed. He frowned at the short line of red brake lights. An accident? No, he realized as the line slowly sped up again. A large crack in the road.

He whistled as he carefully maneuvered around the broken asphalt, already reaching for the radio affixed to the underside of his dashboard. He'd report the treacherous fracture before—

The cell in the seat beside him burst into a funky, retro beat.

He snatched it up, clicked it on. "May Day, what's wrong?"

"God, Dad, why do you have to call me that?"

Annoyed as it was, the sullen tones of his daughter's exasperation cleared a knot from his chest. He exhaled with relief. "Right, right. Everything okay?"

"Yeah, sure. Why?"

"No earthquakes up in Bellingham?" The line cracked noisily, and he grimaced. "Don't pop your gum in my ear," he added mildly.

"Sorry." She didn't sound like she meant it, but at fourteen going on twenty, he'd take what she could give. "There was a small one," she added. "Like, nothing big. Nothing even broke."

Another edge of anxiety loosened. "You sound disappointed," he teased. "Tell me it at least opened up a crack and swallowed your grandmother's taco meat terrier."

She laughed before she remembered she was supposed to be too cool for Dad. "Nope. Boring."

He grinned. "What are you doing up so late, anyway?"

"Movie night at Gram's," she replied. "We watched a zombie flick." Oh, great. Like she didn't have nightmares already. He winced. "We just saw the news and Mom said I should call. She wants to talk to you."

Son of a bitch. "Okay," he said calmly. "Sure. Hey, May Day?"

She groaned. "Dad."

"Love you. See you this weekend, okay?"

"Yeah, whatever." She hesitated. "Hey."

"What's up, kiddo?"

"Um . . . Love you, too, Dad." A sudden feminine voice behind Maylene's cut in, and she added quickly, "Here's Mom."

He guided the car through the thinning traffic as he registered the muffled sound of voices on the other end of the line. Finally, Laura Granger said, "Nigel?"

It didn't matter how long ago they'd separated. Her pretty Southern twang was a kick to his still bruised heart. "Hey, Laura," he said easily. "How's Bellingham?"

"Rattled," she said. "But it's in one piece. I heard Seattle got hit pretty hard. It's all over the news. Are you all right?"

"Everything's fine." He turned into the station parking lot, slowing dramatically to skirt around a scattered mass of old concrete. "There's a little damage, but it's not nearly as bad as they get."

"Right. Okay, well." She trailed off.

Nigel bypassed rows of police cars and navigated into a

parking space. "I'll be over around ten on Saturday," he said, stepping out. "Can you get Lene packed in time?"

"About that."

"Don't you—"

Laura spoke quickly. "I want to stay up here for a few more days. Mom's doing much better and I want Maylene to have some extra time with her."

He slammed the door. "Damn it, Laura, you know how much I've been looking forward to this."

"Really?" Her tone sharpened. "Is that why you canceled the last three weekends?"

His fist clenched around the cell's metal frame. "That wasn't my fault. I'm in the middle of a case—"

"Well, what do you know? Life goes on even when Detective Ferris is on a case," Laura cut in. Her melted butter Southern accent turned to acid real quick. He'd learned that, too. But then it gentled with a sigh. "Look, I know it's not ideal, but I . . . I really think Lene should say good-bye to her grandmother before it's too late. *And* I don't like the fact that Seattle's rockin' like that."

"It was a tiny earthquake, Laura," he said from between his teeth. The parking lot lights flickered as he strode towards the station. "And your mom isn't that old. Come on, don't punish Lene because you're trying to get one up on me."

She sighed again. "That's just it," she said quietly. "This isn't about you at all."

"Laura—"

"Good-bye, Nigel." The line went dead in his ear. He snapped the case shut, jammed it into his pocket, and lengthened his stride.

Fuck it. He'd call back at a decent hour, when they *both* had time to simmer.

The station house was five stories of old mortar and brick, and his floor was on the fourth. Vice shared space with homicide, given the two usually went hand in hand in Seattle.

Maybe it said something that he could easily school his features away from looking angry. It seemed anger was all he ever felt after talking with the mother of his child.

He nodded pleasantly to the desk officers he passed, even managed a little small talk in the stairwell. Not that it mattered. Everyone was talking about the quake. Or, more precisely, the elevator that no one dared to risk with the tremors fresh in everyone's mind.

He pushed the doors open to a cacophony of phones ringing, voices chattering, radios squawking. Stepping into the fourth floor maze of desks, he made a face as a telephone exploded into a wild flurry of bells beside him.

The pretty desk clerk picked it up with a harried look. "Seattle Police, Vice. How can I help you?" He watched Stacey Burke put a hand to her forehead as she added, "No, ma'am, this is the Vice department. You'll need to contact the front desk . . . Yes, ma'am, I'm aware, but the Paris storm was two years ago. No, I don't think it's the same thing." She shot him a helpless grimace as he passed her desk.

"What the hell?" Nigel shrugged out of his jacket, draping it onto his desk chair. "Since when did Vice and Homicide cover the front desk?"

"Since the earthquake scared half the city stupid." Officer Jake Leigh slid a cup of black coffee onto Nigel's desk. "All the doomsdayers are comparing it to Paris and Florida."

Nigel shook his head at the lanky, clean-cut patrolman. Jake could have been the poster boy for the force, with his sandy blond hair and clear blue eyes. Not only was he happily married—the schmuck—but he'd managed to hang onto his wife long enough to get one kid in kindergarten and have another on the way.

"A few cities take a hit and it's the end of the world," he said, grumpy as hell. "What's the damage out there?"

"The usual, after something like this. We all got put on double shifts, too." Jake rubbed at his face. "To be fair, that storm practically swept Paris off the map."

"One disaster years ago doesn't make a trend," Nigel countered evenly.

"Florida?"

"Hurricane central," he said, rolling his eyes. "Give me something we haven't been watching for centuries. Hey, have you heard from Nancy?"

It was like turning on a fucking switch. Jake's whole face lit up at the mention of his wife. "She's shaken, but as they say, no stopping Mother Nature. That baby's due any minute, so Lydia's staying with her mom at the hospital."

"Does she have someone to watch her?"

Jake nodded. "Nancy's sister is there. Good thing, too. Lydia's been having nightmares for the past week, she refuses to sleep alone now."

Sympathy flickered. "Bad ones?"

"I think she's worried the house is going to burn down while we're all sleeping," Jake admitted, rubbing at his forehead. "She keeps saying that the walls are going to fall down. The kid's six and already worrying herself into gray hair, I swear to God. Did your kid go through this?"

Nigel laughed. "Lene's got an imagination worthy of a horror show. I go through it every time she stays over. Try getting Lydia a nightlight? They make some great colorful ones."

"Once the baby's born," Jake said with a rueful grin. "We promised her she could pick out any kind she wanted. Should be any day now, anyway. Doctors are talking induced labor if the kid doesn't ante up soon."

Nigel glanced down at the cup still in his hand. "Hell, just give her some of the station brew," he said wryly. "It'll do all the work at a fraction of the cost." He took a shot of the bitter coffee. It scalded the roof of his mouth. "Son of a—Hot!"

"Yeah," Jake said on a crack of laughter. "Right out of the pot." He paused. "By the way, Chief said to send you in when you showed up."

"Why?"

Jake shrugged, already setting his uniform cap over his combed back hair. "I'm out. I've got all the dispatchers aware to let me know the instant my wife sends out the alert."

"We've got your back." Nigel waved at the cacophony around him as if he could make it disappear. "Come hell or high water."

The officer grinned. Nigel carefully balanced his coffee cup and strode for the far offices.

"Anyone seen the chief?" he asked.

Detective Anderson Waters, one half of Vice's second team and four years away from retiring to a golf course for the rest of his life, gestured down the hall. The phone glued to his ear, he mouthed, "Bitch," and rolled his gray eyes.

The veteran wasn't calling the chief a bitch—though Waters wouldn't have been the first. Nigel scowled as he nodded his thanks.

Bitch without any context could only mean one thing.

He rapped smartly on the chief's office door, waited all of half a second and pushed in.

The tableau was easy to decipher. Station Chief Shannon McClintock sat at her desk, her black hair pulled into a severe knot and her spine ramrod straight. Looming over her, and practically screaming *bitch* from the top of her no-nonsense brunette bob to the tips of her plain black pumps, Sergeant Bethany Simmons leaned her weight on her splayed palms and did her level best to stare down the toughest woman Nigel had ever met.

A lady didn't get to be a police station chief by looking pretty.

Then again, he'd always suspected Simmons had more to offer Internal Affairs than an ice bitch complex. Maybe it had something to do with her terrier-like tenacity.

"Am I interrupting?" he asked, and didn't bother waiting for the answer. He shut the door behind him. "Sorry I'm late, Chief, but there's a hole in my usual route."

Chief McClintock's lips twitched. A smile she hid as she said quietly, "Detective Ferris, I'm sure you've met Sergeant Simmons."

"Never on formal grounds." He gave the Internal Affairs sergeant a smile made of teeth. "Sergeant."

She didn't bother wasting her breath. "We're having a private conversation, detective. If you'd—"

"Right, sure. But my appointment precedes yours," Nigel cut in. He set his cup down on the chief's desk, straight-faced, and added, "There's your coffee, ma'am."

"*You* are late for your appointment," Simmons pointed out coolly.

"Yup." Nigel met her green eyes. They narrowed. "That's what happens when you go out and do real police work. Life gets in the way. Give it a try some time."

The chief stirred. "Detective."

He turned to McClintock. "There's at least seven girls at the halfway house. All immigrants, and not a single green card among them. Every single one is Slavic, I'll stake my badge on it." He ignored Simmons's snort. "They've only got one guard, but I saw cameras, the kind of locks that don't open without a key, and they're scared enough to obey whatever order they're told. That makes at least four operations that we know of in Renton."

The chief rubbed at her forehead. "Any sign of Mikoyan?"

And the kicker. "No," he admitted.

"Waste of time," Simmons said flatly. It sounded like the reiteration of an ongoing argument.

One he didn't want rehashed while he still felt like putting his boot somewhere painful. But that was the job.

"Hardly," he said evenly. "Over the past six months, I've gotten in with the Mikoyan crowd. They've seen what I can bring. They trust me now."

"To what end?" Simmons demanded, despite the fact Nigel directed every earnest word to the chief.

His jaw locked. "Five brothels, four in Renton alone. One,"

he added pointedly, "right here in Bellevue. Two restaurants, one club, and a handful of dockside operations. My money's on laundering." He paused. "So is theirs."

"Can you get us probable cause?" McClintock asked.

"With some effort," Nigel said, nodding. "I can get it for the house right now, if you want, but that's just one operation. Give me enough time, and I'll get you inside Mikoyan's door. Especially since they believe I'm a dirty cop."

This time, he bristled at Simmons's none-too-subtle snort.

He turned his head, bracing his fingertips ever so pointedly on the desk. "You have something to say, Sergeant?"

She folded her arms over her chest. "What's this trust cost us, Ferris?"

He hesitated.

She didn't need his facts. She had her own. "We've handed over too many investigations to this case. They've been allowed to skate when we could have at *least* two of Mikoyan's lieutenants behind bars."

"We needed to give them something," he argued. "What do you suggest? That we grab those two and let the boss walk free? He'll get more. He's got a gang full of mooks ready and willing to do whatever it takes, and if we clear out the head nutcases, it'll be open tryouts all over this city."

She flicked that away. "We're losing face by the hour," she told the chief. "You've let too many cases slip through your fingers, and even though you've assured us that it's all part of the plan, all *I'm* seeing is a cop dealing information for a quick visit to a whorehouse."

A sudden surge of violence surprised Nigel. He found himself taking a step forward, fists clenched.

"Detective."

Every muscle locked. He dragged his glare away from the sergeant's cool challenge. "Yes, chief?" he said, half on a growl.

"Grab a chair." Chief McClintock pinned Simmons with a heavy stare. "I'll talk to *you* when I've heard the report."

"But—"

"In other words, Bethany, get the hell out of my office."

Nigel watched Simmons straighten with icy precision. Her lips sealed into a thin line, she strode for the door, her shoulders rigid.

The door clicked shut behind her, and he relaxed. A little.

The chief scraped both hands over her face. "She's not wrong," she sighed. "Did we make the right call?"

"You know we did," he replied flatly. "I'm not that far from busting this wide open. I'm telling you, we're so much closer than we were six months ago."

"Six months ago," the chief said dryly, "you were fighting this assignment tooth and nail."

Six months ago, he hadn't met Katya.

Which reminded him. "Hey, there was a woman in here this morning." He paused. "Yesterday morning."

She shook her head. "You're going to have to be more specific. Drunk, drugs, or prostitution charge?"

"None of the above . . . I think."

She raised a black eyebrow.

"She was in your office, Shannon. About five-two," he added. "Light blonde hair, blue eyes. Russian as they come, got an accent like it's made of vodka—What?"

McClintock's gaze narrowed. "Hair past her shoulders? About a hundred and twenty pounds, most of it hips and rack?"

And how. "Yup."

She sighed. "Her accent's not that thick. She speaks better English than half my beat cops." She stood, pushing the chair back from the desk. "Her name's Ekaterina Zhuvova."

His brow furrowed. "Is she an informant? A plant, something I should be *aware* of, here?"

The chief hesitated. "No," she said slowly. "She's an immigrant, no green card to speak of and no family. She came here looking for a bargain."

Nigel stared at her. "And you didn't think to tell me about this?"

She straightened, meeting his incredulous stare with a steely one of her own. "She wanted us to move in. I declined. You know the drill, Ferris."

"So what'd you do?" he demanded. "Send her back to that shithole? Pat her on the head and assure her putting out for money is a viable career option?"

McClintock's mouth tightened. "She's a Good fucking Samaritan with a shaky grasp on the law. We could have fished her out, like you said, but Mikoyan would go so far underground, we'd lose him for years."

"For fuck's sake, Shannon."

"Jesus have mercy," she sighed. But it wasn't a prayer for help. The chief slammed a folder closed on her desk, tossing it heedlessly into her overflowing inbox. "Look, she's no different than any of these other girls you're trying to save, right?"

He slammed a hand on the desk. "That's not—"

"It's exactly the point," she cut in smoothly. "You bide your time. You get in good with her, if it'll make you feel better," she added with narrow-eyed scrutiny. "Tuck her under your dirty cop wing, but you get your ass in there and do your job."

Nigel snapped his teeth shut on a vicious rejoinder. "Yes, ma'am."

She frowned. "Don't screw this up, Ferris. You're one clouded decision from being found in a dumpster with a new smile. These guys are for real."

So was he. He rose. "Fine. I'll get you that evidence."

The chief sat back, sighing. "Have patience, Nigel. I know this isn't easy."

Easy, nothing. It was long past any conception of *easy*.

"Yes, ma'am," he said tightly.

"Good. Get out." She sat back into the worn, creaking office chair and closed her eyes. Nigel gave her a minute, crossing the office and waiting with his hand on the door knob. Finally, taking a deep breath, she added, "And send the bitch in."

He hid a grim smile. "Chief wants to see you," he said curtly as he passed Simmons in the hall.

She ignored him.

As he rounded the corner into the cacophony of telephones and voices, Waters flipped a two-fingered salute. "Chief said you're to type up everything before you leave tonight."

Nigel bit back a groan. Of course she had. Anything else she wanted to smack him with? "What's a guy gotta do to get a decent cup of coffee around here?"

Waters grinned. "Don't press your luck, kid."

Chapter Three

"Was he handsome?"

Smothering a yawn, Katya deftly flipped the small, plain pancakes on the griddle. The morning had come too quickly for Katya's liking. Last night's earthquake shook plaster and dust all over the house, and Ivan insisted they clean before they were allowed to sleep.

It had given Katya a chance to reassure them all one more time as they swept and mopped and dusted, but the fitful sleep she'd gotten didn't make her feel better about any of it. The nightmares hadn't stopped, just getting worse and worse every time she rolled over.

Each one featured earthquakes. Fires. Corpses.

Katya rubbed her face. Dreams were funny business. She knew it was just her subconscious translating her fears, but it didn't make it any less frightening.

Especially when the real world pulled a page from her subconscious. The earthquake had been frighteningly intense. And right before their great escape plan, too.

On the plus side, Mother Nature had saved her from one last tumble with a dirty cop.

"Not really," she finally said in returned Russian, her spatula flashing as she swatted away Junie's curious finger. "He was unshaved, and he kept scowling the whole time."

Junie hid a grin.

Leaning against the doorjamb, Elena met Katya's eyes. She was the oldest, maybe twenty-five. Maybe a little more. She was striking enough, with her chemically red hair and curvaceous figure. Irina propped herself up on the slanted, scored counter, her lashes heavy with lack of sleep. She'd entertained clients most of the night. Even after the quake.

Magda and Uliana sat at the flimsy card table, each with a cup of the terrible canned coffee that was all they had.

Elena inhaled a drag from her cigarette, blowing out the smoke to the side—one of the concessions she'd made when she'd befriended Katya, who hated the smell. Her blue eyes gleamed wickedly. "Was he big, at least? He seemed like he'd be big. And very good with his hands."

It was all just chatter. Empty of meaning or intent. All of them knew the plan: escape. Soon, Ivan would come in for a cup of coffee and maybe some of the food she cooked. She'd give him his mug, slip all of the sleeping pills she'd managed to beg from a particularly infatuated john into the hot, bitter brew, and then wait for it to take effect.

It wasn't foolproof, but it was all they had. The rest would burn down with the house when they left.

If they were lucky, so would he.

The thought didn't set well in the bile filling her throat.

"I don't know," she replied patiently, but she avoided Elena's gaze as her ears burned, sidestepping Junie and retrieving a cracked and broken mug from the doorless cabinet above her head. "The earthquake happened. He left immediately." But he'd had good hands, she silently admitted to herself as she poured the weak black coffee into the mug. "Junie, for the last time, get your fingers out of there."

A clatter of plastic made her smile.

"Was he scared when the walls shook, Katya?" The thirteen-year-old popped the stolen batter into her mouth, her brown eyes wide. The childlike gesture kicked Katya in the chest.

Looking at Junie always did.

"No," Katya admitted. "He pushed me to the floor and made sure nothing fell on me." With his body, no less.

"Mine leapt up," Magda said, her nose wrinkled over her coffee mug. "His pants fell down around his ankles and he slid down the stairs like a fat, greased pig."

"Ivan screamed like a little girl." Behind her, Elena chuckled. "He threw himself under the door frame and shook worse than the television."

They all laughed, even if a hint of panic clung to the sound.

Junie wiped her hand on her sweater. "Was he kind, Katya?"

Not even the hardened Elena had the heart to laugh at Junie's question. Naive as it was.

Katya turned, briefly meeting Elena's steady gaze over the girl's platinum blonde head. Her mouth twisted. "They rarely are, sweetheart," Katya said quietly.

The thirteen-year-old nodded, looking away.

A bit more of Katya's heart turned to dust.

She didn't have to say it. Junie knew. Oh, how she knew. Setting her jaw, Katya turned back to the stove. "Who is hungry?" she asked, striving for cheerful. "We must eat now before—"

A door slammed upstairs. Junie jumped, scurrying to Uliana's side, who calmly tucked an arm around her thin shoulders. As Katya's hand froze over the pan, a masculine voice rang through the tiny house.

The angry spate of Russian didn't bode well.

Irina pushed herself upright, her cheeks pale. "He's up," she squeaked fearfully. "He sounds so angry! What do we—"

"Quiet, Irina!" hissed Elena.

Katya's fingers spasmed around the spatula. Then, very calmly, she beckoned the redhead forward. "He does sound angry," she murmured. "He's in a mood, you think?"

Elena nodded grimly.

Ivan's moods were a thing to be feared. They always ended in blood, or tears. Katya took a slow, deep breath. "I will get him his coffee. Whatever happens, you make sure everyone gets out. The van is—"

"I know where it is," Elena said irritably, but her hand touched the small of Katya's back. Silent comfort.

The redhead had seen Katya do this so many times before.

"We will need the keys to get out."

"Break a window, if you have to," Katya told her quietly. "We have to make it to the station on time."

Elena nodded, and turned away.

Her teeth clenched against the anxiety crawling through her skin, Katya headed for the door.

But she wasn't fast enough to intercept him.

Ivan filled the frame, jowls quivering, face mottled.

She stopped short. "You want cof—"

He didn't give her a chance to complete her calculated interception. A meaty fist slammed into her cheek, sending her careening into the scuffed and stained refrigerator. Her head recoiled from it like a muted bell; her ears filled with the echoing rebound.

The girls scattered like a swarm of moths. Junie screamed.

Katya clambered to her knees, forcing herself upright. Gripping the refrigerator handle for support, she spat out Russian curses, thick with pain.

And with fear.

Ivan hovered over her, hands clenching and unclenching. Behind him, Elena pushed Junie out of the kitchen. The others had vanished.

Elena met her eyes, her lips thinned to a fine red line, and crossed herself.

Then she was gone.

Katya's cheek ached. Sweat blossomed across her back as Ivan settled to his thick haunches in front of her. "Now," he said in guttural Russian. "You tell me what I want to know."

She drew her legs in, fingers aching around the handle, but she didn't let herself cringe. Better her than Uliana. Than Junie. She'd watched them cart away the little girl too many times.

She raised her chin.

He stared at her. "The new man. What is his name?"

Katya shook her head. "He didn't tell me."

Ivan's hand shot forward, and she flinched away as it connected with the refrigerator door by her head. "*Lie.* What did he tell you?"

"*Nyet!*" Oh, shit. Oh, shit. Oh—

"What are his likes?"

She swallowed hard, huddling against the cold panel. "Plain," she lied. Ivan's brown-green eyes narrowed. "But he likes words," she added quickly. Not so much a lie. She'd felt his response to her aggression. "I was talking dirty while—"

"You *lie*."

"No!"

Ivan's fist found her mouth, this time. Her head snapped around. Her lip split with almost audible ferocity, and she tasted blood on her tongue. Pain shredded through her head like shrapnel.

I can do this.

No, she couldn't.

"Why were you at the police house?" Ivan growled, breathing heavily.

She jerked.

Oh, *shit*. Had the cop told Ivan?

It was too late to cover her startled tell. Ivan grabbed her by the throat, forcing her up against the refrigerator. Her hair caught on the broken handle, snagging painfully, and she bit back a cry of pain as his fingers gouged into her windpipe.

She couldn't breathe.

He didn't care. "I just received a call," he growled, inches from her face. She gasped for air; he didn't allow her any. "You were *seen*, you little bitch. What were you doing?"

Katya clawed at his grip as her skull filled with pressure. Her lungs cramped, seizing, desperately clamoring for air.

As if she were made of nothing at all, he flicked his hand. The kitchen reeled around her as she sailed across the floor. Her head rammed into the stove; metal shuddered.

Shaking from head to toe, it was all she could do to suck in air through her abused throat. She grabbed the oven handle for balance as she struggled to get to her knees.

But he was there, filling up every inch of space in the kitchen. Katya wrenched at his grip as she caught her by the hair, screaming.

Ivan slammed her to the stovetop, pushed her down until the burner was just under her face. Elena hadn't turned it off; she'd only moved the pan to save the pancakes. The medium heat wafted against her cheek; it made her eyes sting and water.

"Please!" she begged. "I was picked up when I went to the store!" The lies came hard and fast, pouring out of her. "I didn't know why, but they only asked questions and I lied like we should." *Please, oh, God, please . . .*

"What did you tell them?" Ivan's hand flattened on her head, forced her cheek closer to the burner. Closer still. The coiled metal plate blurred under her eye. Her back strained, every muscle in her shoulders and arms and neck screaming as she fought his powerful grip.

"Nothing," Katya sobbed. She didn't have to fake her tears. One plopped on the burner, sizzled, smoked. "I told them I was staying with my sister and I did not work. Please, oh, please, believe me, I swear I told them nothing!"

His grip eased. Katya straightened so fast, the world around her flipped, but there was no time for relief. Ivan grabbed one hand, forced it behind her and pulled up hard enough that her shoulder popped. She screamed, gasping with it as he slammed her back against the stove.

"You are *lying*."

"No," she sobbed, but he wasn't listening. He didn't care. The realization sunk in on a tide of icy clarity.

Someone had sold her out. The dirty cop?

Who else?

"This is only a taste of what happens to disobedient girls," Ivan said over her. His hips pushed into her backside, pinning her to the stove's edge. He'd shifted her away from the burner, but only just barely. She flinched as her elbow came down hard beside it, her skin warming alarmingly fast.

Flinched again as the obvious ridge of his erection pushed against her, hard enough to bruise.

Shame, terror, anger, and pain all gathered in her head. Her chest, her soul.

But it wasn't the first time she'd ever been forced like this. He wasn't the first man who'd ever hit her, or used her, or wanted her to lie to him. The price was high, but the payoff—freedom for her, for the other women—would be worth it.

It had to be. They didn't have anyone else to help them.

She had to persevere.

Katya bit her lip as Ivan reached between them. As she heard the clank and hiss of a belt and zipper. Bit it harder as his fingers wrenched at the buttons of her jeans.

She'd endure this one more time. When he was spent and satisfied, she'd bring him a cup of drugged coffee.

Beneath her tear-filled eyes, four dislodged pancakes cooled on a flat pan.

He was nearly to the Renton brothel when the road shifted out from under him.

Nigel's SUV skidded across the wet asphalt, the ground flipped and rolled like a serpent, and it was all he could do to grab the wheel with both hands and fight to keep the car from sliding sideways.

Horns blasted. Metal crunched as drivers careened into

poles, parked cars and each other. A boxy four-door slammed into the back of his vehicle. He swore desperately as he shot into a tailspin that carried his car across two lanes, narrowly missing a taxi and slamming into the side of a parked station wagon. Its windshield shattered.

Vibrations rippled through Nigel's feet, the seats. Cautiously unpeeling his sweat-damp fingers from the steering wheel, he very carefully engaged his emergency brake.

That was close.

Brick clattered to the ground outside his window.

His heart began to slow from its frenetic pace, letting him suck in a deep, steadying breath. Too damned close. Thank God there'd been time to—

The ground rumbled. The street reared in front of him.

It shuddered, rolling side to side, and Nigel slammed into the driver's side door as the see-saw motion pitched him backwards. He cursed, grabbed the wheel for balance and froze.

A line of cars suddenly vanished.

His car shook violently. He heard screaming, watched a surge of people running toward him; away from the disappearing road.

No. Not disappearing.

Sinking.

"Jesus Christ!" Nigel jerked the locks up, manually forcing the mechanism free, and half-spilled out of the trembling car. The ground pitched wildly. The door slammed closed with the momentum, mere millimeters from his fingers.

Cars bounced and slid like toys on a rickety table.

"Run!" he shouted. He grabbed a teenager shocked into stillness, shoved him forward as he ran back the way he'd driven.

The kid stumbled, his earphones falling out of his hoodie, and Nigel grabbed him bodily around the waist, swinging him half over his shoulder as he sprinted away from the trench rapidly gaining ground.

The buildings swayed dangerously, shrapnel clattered to the ground; brick, cement, glass, and wood. Shrieks filled the air, drowned out by the ear-shattering crack of crumbling rock as the street all but vanished behind him.

The screams filled his head. His bones.

Dust billowed into the air, a cloud of choking debris. And then, as suddenly as it started, everything fell still.

The tremors stopped, the ground settled.

Remnants of old mortar and loose brick clattered to the street. There was a moment of raw, terrible silence, and then voices rose again. Shocked, this time. Helpless and frightened.

Nigel put the teenager down. "You okay?"

The kid stared at him, wide-eyed. No, not at him, Nigel realized. Behind him.

He turned.

However long the street used to be, it'd just gained another twenty-three yards.

"Holy fuck," the kid whispered hoarsely.

The skeleton of buildings caught along the ledge of the newly formed chasm hung listlessly over the side, as if sawed in half. Sparks flickered from torn wires and loose beams.

Cars hung half over the edge. People stared, sobbed. Screamed for help.

And on the other side of that hole in the earth, a dust cloud roiled. It came from the same neighborhood as Katya's prison.

"Son of a bitch!"

Nigel took off, already retrieving his cell from the clip on his belt. "Call Maylene Granger," he said into the voice command. It dialed, and as he waited for it to connect, he sprinted across the street. Into an alley and around the block.

The line rang. And rang.

"Come on, come on," he muttered through clenched teeth. He dodged the scrambling crowds, bypassed huddled people staring at the wreckage of their shaken buildings. Debris cluttered the roads and sidewalks, but there was nothing like the trench that had just swallowed his car.

"Damn it!" He punched a button. "Call *work*."

The phone hit a busy signal.

"Fuck!" Nigel clipped his cell to his belt, lowered his head and concentrated on running like hell to the squat neighborhood with its cloud of dust.

The block wasn't built for earthquakes. Buildings lay in heaps as he barreled down the sidewalk. People gathered, ambulances were already on the scene—a small consolation. He saw bloody faces and rubble where homes used to be.

He saw cars crunched together, soldered by the impact, and as he rounded the corner, he saw a knot of women all holding each other outside the skeleton of a broken-down house. Familiar women.

Familiar fucking house.

But no Katya.

He staggered to a halt beside them, grabbing a redhead by the arm. "Where's Katya?" he demanded.

She pointed a shaking finger at the house. Dust smudged her cheek, coated the others' hair and clothing. "Inside," she said in thick English. "She is inside. We called and called!"

"Katya," sobbed a girl that couldn't have been much older than his own daughter.

Nigel gritted his teeth. "Cross the street," he ordered. "All of you, get away from the house. I'll be right out. Don't—" A gunshot splintered the air.

It echoed like a sonic boom in the stillness that followed.

"Katya!" shrieked the little girl.

He sprinted toward the house. He didn't bother with the front door—the whole living room had torn open, exposed to the street behind him and covered in plaster and insulation so old it disintegrated.

He grabbed the gun from his shoulder holster, held it as he cleared the living room. The hall. His feet crunched on the remnants of walls and ceiling. "Katya?" he called. "Ekaterina!"

The destruction only made the house look like a dollhouse gone to hell.

Flinching as the light fixture cracked and sparked, he hurried down the hall and burst through the kitchen archway. "Katya—"

He careened to a stop, one arm holding his Beretta steady even as he found himself staring down the barrel of a very large Desert Eagle.

Like David versus Goliath, but with guns. *Jesus Christ.*

He straightened slowly, met glazed blue eyes over the unsteady weapon. "Put the gun down, Katya."

She was covered in plaster dust, her hair tangled and T-shirt filthy. Blood smeared across her cheek. Oozed sluggishly from a cut at her lower lip. The dust turned it nearly black.

The bruise swelling her right cheek kicked concern into a vicious need for violence. Who the *fuck* had put his hands on her?

In a brothel? *Everybody.*

He lowered his gun. "Katya, it's Nigel. Remember me?"

Her blue eyes flickered.

"I'm police, remember? It's okay. You're safe. I'm not going to hurt you."

The gun in her straining arms lowered slowly. "You . . . Truth."

What? He frowned. A glance around the ruined, cluttered kitchen was enough to tell him what happened. The man who had brokered the deal with Nigel the day before lay on the floor, his chest crimson. A griddle pan lay upended beside him, and what looked like half a torn pancake flopped in the scuffed rubble strewn across the floor.

Katya's jeans were unfastened, askew enough to reveal a twisted lavender swatch of cheap-looking lace and a glimpse of golden hair.

That fucking *bastard.*

Blood splattered her T-shirt. Her blood, Ivan's; Nigel didn't know. He hoped to hell it was Ivan's. The son of a bitch.

It took monumental effort to force his voice to calm. "It's okay. It's over." He holstered his gun, splayed his hands. "Come on, we need to get you out of here."

She blinked slowly. As if focusing on him through a heavy fog. "Out . . . The girls? Are they safe? Did they get out?"

Her accent wasn't nearly so pronounced today. Despite the violence struggling for dominance in his skin, despite the corpse he desperately wanted to plug full of holes for what Ivan had done—tried to do?—to her, he couldn't help a faint, wry smile.

The little liar.

"They're safe," he told her, ignoring her miraculously improved English. "Just give me the gun."

Much to his surprise, she didn't argue. Reversing her grip on the Desert Eagle, much too large for her small hands, she offered the weapon.

Her eyes, still filled with shock, settled on the corpse at her feet. "He . . . I—" Her voice broke.

"It's okay," he said softly, removing the gun from her outstretched hands. "He won't hurt you again. Fix your jeans, Katya."

She looked down at herself. At her bloodstained T-shirt and the obvious evidence of what she'd just gone through, and her cheeks reddened. Quickly, with shaking fingers, she fastened the buttons. "Nothing happened," she said quickly. "I hit him."

"Good girl." He took her hand before she could withdraw. "The others are waiting for you. Let's go—"

The black and white tile cracked. Katya staggered as the kitchen floor shifted beneath her, and Nigel swore. Hauling on her hand, he ordered, "Get out!"

She moved fast, for a civilian. As if shaking off whatever fog of shock clung to her, she sprinted for the door. He gripped her hand tight, helped her when she stumbled, handed her through the fallen wall and started across the street.

She stopped. "We have a van." She let go of his hand, darted down the sidewalk; her arms splayed for balance as the cement bucked beneath her.

"Katya, damn it!" Nigel whistled loud enough that the sound pierced through the rumble. The women saw him, screamed too much for him to decipher.

He waved them over. "Get to the van," he roared. "Go."

Thank God, they knew where it was. Katya beat them all to it, warmed the engine. As Nigel followed them, the shuddering tremors slammed into overdrive, pitching the ground this way and that. The house collapsed behind him, joined by the structures on each side.

The redhead opened the back doors, helped the women inside. "In, in," she yelled, gesturing at Nigel.

He rounded the front of the battered white vehicle, wrenched open the front door and half-pushed, half-lifted Katya across the front seat. "I drive," he said tersely, and threw the vehicle into gear.

The damned dust cloud exploded into a field of debris as he slammed the gas pedal to the floor.

Chapter Four

They were out. Somehow, miraculously, they'd been rescued.

Rescued, for God's sake. *Ved'ma* or not, she never could have foreseen this.

Katya rested her chin on Junie's head and inhaled the fragrance of her flaxen hair. Soap and dust and the remnants of cheap perfume.

It was almost normal.

Except for the chaos on the streets around them and the fact that a dirty cop was driving Ivan's van. Dead Ivan. She hadn't even needed the sleeping pills.

She muffled a hysterical giggle against Junie's hair. The girl's death grip on her waist tightened.

Scared. And Katya couldn't blame her. For the past ten minutes, since the instant the van had pulled away from the fractured curb, they'd all been tense and silent. Waiting for the other shoe to drop, maybe.

She watched Nigel punch in another series of numbers into his cell. Whomever her unwitting savior was calling, he wasn't happy about it. Frowning, Nigel put the cell down, once more replacing his hands on the wheel.

The scene outside was nothing short of pandemonium. People wandered, some bruised and filthy. Fires had started near downed power lines. A sheet of water gushed from a hydrant bent nearly in half under a car half jacked on top of it, pounding the roof as they drove under its spray.

The radio in the van droned quietly. "Sources say Alaska's Mount Redoubt erupted around two in the morning," the pert female voice said. "Shockwaves were felt as far south as Olympia, though authorities don't expect these to continue past the next day or so. Experts, however, are predicting a sudden temperature decrease by up to three degrees in the Pacific northwest—"

A rustle of movement drew her attention away from the stern lines of Nigel's face. Elena crouched between the seats, her shiny purple pants stretched taut over her thighs. "You are taking us somewhere safe?" she asked, her accent thick as mud.

Katya rubbed Junie's back softly as the girl stirred.

Nigel didn't look away from the treacherous road he navigated. "To the police station. We have—"

"That is *not* safe," Elena said firmly.

He flicked Katya a glance.

She shrugged.

"I want to go to my son," Elena continued, her tone unshakeable. "He is with others. The girls will come. Katya?"

She hesitated.

"Katya comes with me," Nigel said flatly. And if the redhead's tone was unshakeable, Katya read nothing but steely determination on the cop. She winced.

Elena blinked at her. Then, with a ghost of a smile, she said, "Junie can—"

"I want to stay with Katya," Junie said in sudden, rapid Russian.

"Sweetheart," Katya murmured, as soothing as she could. "I don't think he would like it if—"

"You can stay with Katya," Nigel interrupted in that damned passable Russian of his. She shot him a narrow-eyed glare, but his features were implacably dense.

Determined. Right. She got it.

But he didn't have to let the girl stay. That he did was . . . oddly kind.

Who the hell was he?

Junie settled, burying her face in Katya's shoulder, her back to Nigel. Elena nodded, pleased. She gave the man an address and returned to the back of the van, bracing herself against the lurching momentum.

Katya stroked Junie's back softly. "That was very nice," she said quietly.

He didn't look at her. "She wants to protect her family. I get that."

"And Junie?"

"Is that her name?"

Katya's hand stilled. Then, slowly, she resumed the rhythmic, reassuring caress. "Not likely."

"Is your name really Katya?"

The tone didn't change even an iota. Cool. Calm. Cop voice, she thought, and sighed. "Yes. My name actually is Ekaterina. Katya, for short."

"You speak better English than you let on."

Junie's breath soaked into her shoulder, warm and vitally alive. Holding the girl tightly, Katya leaned her head back against the seat, tried to ignore the dull pain seeping into the side of her face as the adrenaline faded, and studied Nigel's profile.

She'd lied when she told the others that she didn't find him handsome. Although not classically pretty, his features had an arresting quality she found intriguing.

And he hadn't shaved, she noticed.

Her lips curved faintly. "I learned fast." It was the only way to hear the lies in a foreign country.

His fingers tightened on the wheel. "Why were you in that house?"

"Are you a dirty cop?"

He fielded her return volley with raised eyebrows, only now turning his head to meet her forthright stare. His eyes were almost black in the gray daylight. "No," he said flatly. "I'm a good cop pretending to be a dirty cop so that I can take down that son of a bitch Mikoyan."

All conversation stopped behind them.

Truth. She stared at him. "You mean that."

Nigel cursed quietly and concentrated again on the van. The radio droned on. He asked her no more questions, and after that bombshell, she wasn't sure she wanted to pry any more.

Once the others were safe, she'd ask. She'd ask about his case. She'd ask why girls like Junie were abandoned to the system while men like him got to screw them in the name of evidence.

So much anger.

Smoothing back Junie's hair, Katya closed her eyes and let herself doze.

It couldn't have been long. The vehicle slowed suddenly, and a flurry of activity jarred her solidly awake. Junie mumbled something incoherent against her neck, this time really asleep.

Nigel climbed out of the van, circled around the back and unbarred the back doors. Light flooded through the interior.

Katya opened the passenger door and slid out, Junie held awkwardly in her arms. "Elena."

The redhead stretched, her silk tank-top clinging to every curve, and shot Katya a grin from beneath her vivid bangs. "This is freedom, of a kind," she said lazily in her native language.

Katya opened her free arm and she stepped into it, hugging her as warmly as if they were sisters.

"Be safe," Katya instructed sternly. "Get out of Seattle. Go somewhere else." She didn't know why the words seemed so important, but she said them anyway. Seattle wasn't safe anymore.

True enough, anyway, as long as Mikoyan was alive.

"You are too young to be acting like a mother," Elena replied. She tucked a stray tendril of blonde behind Katya's ear, then ran her fingers down Junie's back. "Live your life, now."

It was sweet. But she couldn't promise anything, not as long as there were girls like her.

Katya kissed the women, said her farewells with tears thick in her throat, and returned to the van. Nigel watched silently, the set of his mouth unreadable.

Katya was always so good at reading people. Nigel's blank slate expressions unnerved her.

"I will come soon to talk to you," Nigel said in his cautious grasp of Russian.

Elena looped her arms around Irina and Magda, her smile nothing short of maneating. "You are good man," she replied in English. "But we will not be here."

Nigel hesitated. Then, jaw shifting, he nodded. "Take care of yourselves."

"Da."

"Do svidaniya!" Katya called in farewell. Junie stirred, but slept on. Hiking the girl's lanky body higher into her arms, she touched her fingers to her mouth and blew them all a silent kiss.

Her heart twisted as Nigel shut the door behind her.

As he climbed back into the driver's seat, his gaze touched on her face. Her swelling cheek. Something predatory banked. "Why did Ivan hit you?"

She flinched before she could force herself not to. "Someone told him I'd been to the police."

He swore viciously, too under his breath to catch the specifics. But there was no misreading the leashed tension in his hands, the taut muscles of his arms as he held the steering wheel.

She took a deep breath. "Was it you?" she demanded.

"No. Hell, no," he said tightly, his eyes hard on the traffic-choked road. "But I'm damn well going to find out who."

Truth. On both counts. He believed what he said.

For the moment, it was enough.

She leaned back against the door, once more running gentle fingers down Junie's spine. Her lashes drifted closed, but even as she listened to radio, her mind wouldn't stop spinning.

Ivan was dead. She'd killed him. Her. Katya Zhuvova. She'd never killed a man before in her life, but she'd pulled the trigger.

And he'd fallen.

The disgusting man was going to rape her. To *teach her a lesson*; well, she'd taught *him*, all right. With a frying pan and his own gun.

She squeezed her eyes shut.

"Hey." He sounded so gentle. So damned reassuring.

Was it a sign of weakness that she so badly wanted to be reassured?

"It's going to be okay," he said, and for the first time since meeting him, she detected a lie. But that was all right. Reassurance usually came on the back of a white lie, didn't it?

It was almost enough to make her smile.

"The world is going to hell," she said without opening her eyes. "I really don't think it's going to be okay at all."

He fell silent. And then, after what seemed like an eternity of waiting, he said, "I hope you're wrong."

Ah, her senses whispered. *Truth.*

He was an optimist, this cop.

It took far too long to get to the police station. Traffic backed up across the city, detours were installed around damaged bridges and overpasses. People milled in crowds, ambulances tore through roads shredded by fractures. By the time Nigel had escorted them to a small, clean office, Katya was worn to the bone. Strung out on faded adrenaline and, though she tried to keep from showing it, shaking from head to toe.

An older man with a rumpled suit had tried to ask her questions, but Nigel had deflected him.

He'd left, come back with clean clothes for both herself and Junie, and left again, shutting the office door behind him.

The silhouette of a police man hovered behind the drawn shade.

Katya was grateful. Junie sat on a worn green couch, wearing a too-large T-shirt and curled up into as small a ball as she could make herself.

Katya sat on the floor, her fingers loosely linked around the girl's gangly ankles. Her own borrowed shirt was gray, smelled like Nigel, and hung like a sack on her much shorter frame. "They're going to ask us some questions," she said, meeting Junie's exhausted brown eyes. "When we tell them everything, we'll be free."

Junie's lip quivered. "Will we go back to Ivan?"

Katya flinched. "No, sweetheart. You'll never have to go back to Ivan."

The girl fell silent, her chin on her knees. Her lips worked for a while, as if framing a question.

"What is it?" Katya asked gently.

"That man." Junie's blond eyebrows knotted. "You said he wasn't handsome."

"Did I?"

"Yes." She frowned. "You lied."

Katya smothered a chuckle. "You think so?"

"Yes." Junie's hand lowered. A single finger hooked into Katya's hand. "Do you think he would take me?"

The question, asked in all sincerity, slammed a hole into Katya's heart. Fury pounded behind her eyes; fury that a child should be so conditioned to think that way, and sorrow that she didn't know any other way to think.

Katya closed her eyes, turning her hand palm up to lace her

hand through Junie's. "I think if you ask him, he will be your friend."

A light tap on the door had her standing before she knew she meant to.

"Excuse me." A handsome man in a police uniform leaned through the doorway, one hand on the doorknob. His blue eyes flickered; sympathy, Katya thought. Awareness. He noticed the way Katya stood in front of Junie, and by the twist in his mouth, it bothered him.

Junie rose to her knees, her hand tight in Katya's, and peeked around her.

"My name is Officer Jake Leigh," he offered. "I'm going to make sure you ladies have everything you need. Are you hungry? Thirsty?"

Katya hesitated, glancing over her shoulder. "Hungry, sweetheart?" she asked in Russian.

Junie nodded.

Officer Leigh tilted his head. "Is she all right to come with me? I can escort her to the cafeteria."

And Katya desperately wanted a nap.

"This police man will take you to food," she translated, searching Junie's expression for any sign of fear. "His name is Jake Leigh. Do you want to go with him?"

Junie's gaze flicked to the officer.

He sank to his haunches, draping his elbows on his thighs and somehow making himself look less threatening. "Less big. How do you say hello?" he asked.

"*Privet,*" Katya offered. "Her name is Junie."

Junie ducked her head. Jake matched the gesture, tilting his face up to smile at her. "*Privet,* Junie. Will you come with me? I promise to keep you safe."

He offered one hand, his expression at ease. Infinitely patient.

The door widened behind him, and Nigel stepped in, a folder in hand. He glanced at the officer crouched on the floor and then at the girl kneeling on the couch. Raising his eyebrows, he sidled around the officer to set his folder quietly on the desk.

He said nothing.

Katya looked at Junie, watched uncertainty meld into something cautiously optimistic. "Go on," she murmured in Russian. "I'll be right here."

Junie unfolded from the couch, framing something cautious and impossibly hopeful in Russian.

Jake cocked his head at Katya.

"She wants pancakes," Nigel translated, his voice quiet and smoky.

Jake's smile widened. "*Da,*" he said in his flat American accent. "That's yes, right?"

"*Da,*" Katya confirmed.

Junie cautiously slipped her hand into his.

Katya folded her arms over her chest. "Do you have children, Officer Leigh?"

His eyes warmed. "One," he said. "And one on the way."

"All right," Nigel said irritably. "Get out."

Jake shot him a look filled with laughter, shaking his head, and guided the young teenager out the door. It closed behind them, leaving Katya alone with the man who'd kissed her blind the first time she'd seen him.

And rescued her friends the next.

She blew out a slow, shaking breath, her arms tightening around her ribs.

Nigel flicked on a lamp, adding a little more light to the gray daylight peeking through the blinds. "There was an earthquake in California, too. They say we're getting a series of aftershocks from both ends."

"Really," she whispered.

"It beats the end-of-days scenario every ragtag nutcase with a sign is preaching," he said, his smile crooked.

It faded when she didn't answer. He half outstretched a hand, paused as if unsure whether to approach her or to let her be. "Katya." She flinched. "Are you all right?"

And there it was. That kindness.

The crack.

Her knees folded. Katya hit the floor, hunched over herself, and let her chin sink to her chest. Her breath came in shuddering gasps as the relief, the shock, finally set in. With a vengeance.

He swore, crossing the office so quickly that he was suddenly kneeling beside her, an arm around her shoulders. One under her knees. "Hey, it's okay," he soothed. "I've got you."

He lifted her with a smooth flex of power, transferred her to the sofa and hesitated as her fingers dug into his shirt. "Please," she whispered. Tears filled her eyes; damn it, she wasn't supposed to cry.

It was over. Junie was safe. Elena and the others were going to be free.

Why was she crying?

Nigel looked down at her shaking hands, his features conflicted. Then, as if afraid he might spook her farther, he sank into the sofa cushions beside her. Cautiously lifted her, settling her sideways on his lap as if she were just a child to be comforted.

His body heat seeped into her legs. Her back.

Her cheek as she tucked her face against his shoulder and shook violently.

He stroked her hair with a callused hand. "It's okay," he murmured. His breath stirred against her temple, smelling like mint toothpaste and coffee. "It's going to be okay. You're safe here."

"I kn-know," she said, so tightly her teeth clattered together. "I know. It's just . . . it's . . . *Damn it*."

"Shhh." His arms tightened around her. "There's no shame in letting go."

She almost laughed. It came out on a dry sob.

"I'm going to do everything I can to protect you both," Nigel said. And in that gentleness, she heard a fierce promise. A tenacious aggression that did more to set her mind at ease than any empty reassurances.

Truth, her mind whispered.

"You're witnesses to Mikoyan's operation," he continued, smoothing her hair back from her face as she looked up. His eyes gleamed, inches from her own, and his features were tense, but his touch gentle as he tucked her hair behind her ear. "We'll get your stories, and we'll have more to nail the bastard with when I bring it all down on his head."

She stared into his eyes. Realized she had already started shaking her head when they narrowed.

"No?"

"I just . . . I can't put Junie through that," she said, closing her eyes. "She's just a baby."

"Condition of anonymity," he replied. "As long as the facts are good, they'll never have to know who she is. We'll make them work." He caught her jaw with one hand, long fingers framing her cheeks, and forced her to look at him. To meet his gaze again; see the determination. Drown in it. "You're the bravest lady I know. You can do this."

Brave? She wasn't brave.

She was crazy.

A tear slid from her lashes as she clenched her fists in his collar and pulled his mouth to hers.

Surprise stiffened his body. Maybe it was a sense of propriety, of duty that kept him from kissing her back. Maybe he was thinking that he was a police detective, sworn to protect, and she was the wounded victim of a crime. She didn't know. All she knew was that she wanted to taste Nigel Ferris's kiss again.

And the hoarse sound deep in his throat told her that he remembered hers.

Chapter Five

His lips softened. The arms pushing her way suddenly pulled her closer to him, crushing her breasts against his chest. Pulled her hip awkwardly against his groin, hard beneath his jeans.

He groaned raggedly, the wordless confession welling from deep, deep inside his chest as he caught her face between his hands. As he had before, his thumbs dug in by her mouth. Tilted her face up, forced her lips to open, to surrender to the hot, wet, almost angry insistence of a kiss that rocked her down to her shaking soul.

Her eyes clenched shut, blocking out the small office. The green sofa, the dreary Seattle light. The muted hum of the police station faded beneath the slam of her heartbeat; or was it his? There was only the rasp of his tongue as it slipped into her mouth, teasing hers. Daring hers to meet his fervor, match it.

She inhaled through her nose, a shaky breath flavored with his scent. Sawdust and pine and coffee and, Jesus, sheer lust. She shifted, struggling to keep her lips fused to his. Breathed his breath and tilted her head, rising to her knees.

His hands tightened around her face, and he wrenched his lips away on a low, hoarse word. It sounded like *fuck*.

Smoothly, she hiked a leg over his thighs. Shifted her weight so that her knees framed his hips. His eyes blazed at her, glittered with barely contained need. Raw lust.

"Katya, we can't." His breath hissed through his teeth as she grabbed fistfuls of his shirt at each shoulder and settled herself hard, firmly against his covered erection.

The thick ridge fit exactly where her body craved it. She gasped, bit her lower lip.

The small pain of the cut there wasn't nearly enough to quell her need for his touch. His lips on hers, his fingers on her skin. His cock inside her. It was almost a compulsion.

"Will you make me beg?" she whispered.

He groaned tightly, his hands coming to clasp her waist.

"Please." She tilted her hips. The cleft of her body pulsed, wetter than she ever would have expected from something like this. From a man like him.

From herself.

"Please," she said again. "If it's . . . if it's me you're worried about, I'm healthy. We . . . they check us. Healthy is much more money—"

"No," he rasped, cutting her off with an angry sound. His fingers tightened at her hips. Held her when she would have moved again. "Don't beg. Don't ever beg . . . another man . . ." And then his fingers found the hem of her shirt. Hiked it above her breasts with almost savage need. "No other men," he growled, and lowered his head to the cleavage lifted into place by her pink bra. His tongue tasted the upper swell of one breast and she gasped.

No other men.

It smacked of truth.

Her head fell back as his fingers slid beneath the soft cups cradling her flesh. He pulled the bra down, freeing her breasts to his gaze. He stared at her, at her dusky nipples tightened to hard little buds of wanting.

"Beautiful."

She'd heard it before.

But as he lowered his mouth to one aching nipple, she nearly shot out of her skin with raw lust. That was new.

He lapped at her skin, at her nipple, his other hand palming her other breast with rough, confident strength. She arched into him, crying out softly, just aware of their surroundings enough that she muffled what she could. "Please," she panted, "oh, please."

He laughed, but it was as if it was ripped from him. Nigel pulled her shirt over her head, unclasped her bra until she was topless. The chilly air ghosted over her skin, causing gooseflesh to ripple down her arms. Over her chest.

He seized her hands, held them away from her body. His eyes devoured every inch of her, from her softly rounded stomach to the heavy swell of her breasts. To her eyes. Katya dissolved into a pool of molten sensation as she read awe in his dark eyes.

Admiration.

She made a small sound, wrenched her hands away to tunnel them under his shirt. She wasted no time in tugging the cotton over his head, revealing the tanned, muscled skin of a man at the peak of physical perfection. Her mouth went dry at the ridged expanse of his abs, at the dark hair on his chest and the way his own flat nipples tightened beneath her finger.

His breath caught. "This is such a bad idea," he said, half a laugh. Half a groan.

"Maybe." She met his eyes briefly. Her lips curved up. "Maybe it's exactly the right idea." She bent, licked a path up the center of his chest. Found the thin skin where his shoulder met his neck and bit. Hard.

He almost shot off the couch. "Oh, *fuck*," he growled, and entwined his fingers in her hair. Jerking her back, he fit his mouth to hers, slanted his lips over hers until she groaned from the friction between them. His lips. His cock, still locked away behind the thick layers of denim.

She wrenched at her jeans. The buttons popped open, audibly loud in their feverish scrambling. His zipper hissed. He hooked a thumb in the waistband of his light blue boxers, the front damp with the evidence of his own arousal, and pushed them down, revealing his erection. Paler than the rest of his suntanned skin, but flushed and thick and so tempting that her mouth fell open. She licked her lower lip, panting.

Fire roiled inside her skin; a flush climbed from her core to her flesh, warming her beyond any furnace. Egging her on.

His features were taut with wanting, his muscles pulling and flexing as he grabbed her weight and shifted her just enough that she could wriggle out of her jeans. Her underwear wasn't made of enough material to bother. But instead of climbing up his lap, instead of impaling herself as badly as she wanted it, she turned. Slid off the sofa until her bare knees found the rough carpet and slammed a hand into the center of his chest as he moved.

"Ne dvigat'sya," she ordered, her voice heavy with wanting.

He twitched, but held still.

Her smile deepened to something wicked. Oh, God, she really was crazy.

Her fingernails dug into his chest. He leaned back, every muscle vibrating with the control she read leashed in his eyes, his clenched teeth. Before he could talk, stop her—*try*—she bent over his lap. Closed her lips over the head of his rigid cock, and tasted him as thoroughly as if he were baklava fresh from home.

His head snapped back, cords standing out in his throat as she took him in, deep into her mouth. Her throat. She was practiced, she had to be, but this wasn't like those other times. This wasn't anything like it.

This was her gift. *Her* choice.

His pleasure.

She watched him through her lashes as she sucked at him; thrilled as his hands tunneled into her hair, not to push her away but to guide her. Hold her hair from her face so he could see her mouth work him, suck him, take him in deep, nearly to his balls.

His eyes glittered, painfully bright. His jaw clenched so hard she could see a muscle leap in his jaw.

It echoed the muscle leaping against her throat, her lips.

"Oh, God," Nigel rasped, so hoarse it was nearly nothing more than a whisper. She'd found his tipping point. His fingers tightened around her head and pulled her off, his cock sliding free of her mouth with a soft sucking sound. He grabbed her by the arms and yanked her across his lap.

Katya caught herself against his shoulders. For a moment,

a breath of time, she stiffened. He was aggressive. He was all male, and she'd teased him, but he . . .

He wouldn't hurt her. He couldn't.

He wasn't like *them*.

"Damn." As if aware he'd toed up to some kind of line, he let go of her arms. Although his erection twitched, glistening from her attentions, he didn't move. His eyes pinched, mouth twisting. "I'm sorry. I'm so sorry, I didn't mean—"

Katya settled a finger over his lips. They stilled, but he didn't have to talk to show her what he was thinking. His eyes were filled with it: Regret. Anger. Concern.

She leaned in, replaced her finger with her lips and kissed him so softly that even she shivered with it. "You are you," she said. "You are not—"

Them.

Nigel didn't let her finish. He kissed her again, swallowing the word. The memories. His hands gentler, he stroked them down her back. Over the curve of her ass, framed in lavender lace. She braced one hand on his chest, warm and so alive under her palm, and pulled aside the stretchy swatch of her underwear.

His cock nudged her, and she sucked in a deep, sudden breath.

Everything narrowed down to this second. This moment, his hot flesh against hers. His gaze boring into her own; his hands steady on her waist. Supporting, not restraining. Warm and callused and protective.

Closing her eyes, she sank down, impaled herself with a slow, wet slide of flesh in flesh, and threw her head back on a fierce, satisfied moan.

He echoed it. His fingers dug into her waist, but it was Katya who set the pace. Her will that curved her hips, slid them away, then slammed them back. His length rubbed inside of her, filled her, each inch like a benediction, a healing salve.

There was nothing before Nigel.

There would be nothing after.

Katya knew only now. Her body's temperature rising. Her brain fragmenting as she rode him. Her thighs burned with the effort, but his hands helped her to steady herself; let her concentrate on the fierce intensity of his cock buried deep inside her. In and out. Stroking, stretching, filling.

One of his hands moved. She gripped the arm of the sofa beside them as she struggled to quiet her moans. And then his thumb touched the hard knot of nerves between her swollen folds and that was the end of any pretense of control she had.

She orgasmed on a long, shuddering arc of sensation and sound. It uncoiled like a flood crashing through a shattered dam, rolling through her from head to toe and back again; centered always on his thrusts, on the jerky motion of his hips where they joined. She watched his features tense. "Katya," he gasped.

"Do it," she whispered, and watched his eyes flash and darken and finally close as he came inside her.

It set off every nerve she had. Forced another screaming tide through her body, her chest, her throat. He captured the back of her head in one hand, swallowed her cry with a kiss that filled her mouth as deeply as he still filled her body.

When she couldn't take it anymore, she tore her lips away, gasped for air as her heart slammed against the cage of her ribs.

Nigel's breath came in low, slowing pants. Unable to resist him, she let him tug her down to his chest. Her knees burned from the sofa cushions, her hip was threatening to lock at any moment, but Katya said nothing.

Slowly, closing her eyes and burying her face in his chest, she listened to Nigel's heart pounding beneath her ear. For a long time, neither spoke.

When his heart had slowed, and her breath once more came and went without shaking, Nigel stirred. "You must be hungry."

She didn't bother opening her eyes. "Tired."

His breath stirred the hair over her face as he sighed. "Of course you are." Slowly, as if she were made of glass, he shifted out from under her. The loss of his body heat immediately made her shiver. "I'm going to get you some food," he said, refastening his pants. His features were granite hard. Locked down.

Katya blinked at him. "I . . . Is everything all right?"

He hesitated. His expression gentled, and he bent to hand her the jeans they'd tossed to the floor. When she took them, he caught her hand. "I'm not running away," he said, so seriously that her heart fluttered. "I'm just giving you food. And a chance to . . ." His mouth worked for a moment. Then, helplessly, he gestured at the office. The sofa.

Her. Naked but for a purple thong.

"Get presentable?" she hazarded. But she couldn't help the smile in her voice. Or the warmth slowly filling her chest.

"That," he agreed. He squeezed her fingers, and let her go. "I'll be back. You'll eat, and then catch some sleep. And I'll check on Junie," he promised, before she could even frame the thought in her head.

She watched him leave the office, her mind whirling. As the door swung shut, she saw him scrape both hands through his hair. Like a man beset by trouble.

"So close," she whispered, and looked at the denim clenched in her lap. She was so damned close to making the worst mistake of her life.

Or maybe . . . Katya closed her eyes. Or maybe the best.

Chapter Six

"How is she?"

Nigel looked up from the paperwork he hadn't been writing on for the past hour. It took his bleary vision a long moment to clear, focusing Jake Leigh's double image into one serious expression of concern.

He palmed at his eyes, straightening his back from its half-slump. "She?"

Jake's mouth quirked. "Katya."

"On a first name basis, are you?" Nigel couldn't help the underlying lash of jealousy beneath the wry question. He gouged his thumb into one eye, rubbing as if he could stamp out the fierce, protective surge.

"She's fine," he added before Jake's mouth could frame the question his raised eyebrows were asking. "Sleeping. Her and Junie. I figured I'd give them an hour more before diving into the interrogation portion of our day. We have a few hours before the child welfare advocate arrives."

"Poor kid." The officer leaned against the desk, and for the first time, Nigel saw the shadows under his blue eyes. Lines bracketed his mouth. "That girl . . . It just makes you want to *do* something, you know?"

Oh, yeah. He knew. He'd done something, all right. He sighed, pushing aside the sheaf of papers. "You can't fix the world, Leigh."

"Yeah, well. I sure want to try."

Nigel smiled wearily. "That's why you've got a badge. Any word from Nancy?" He deftly served the change of subject before either of them could dwell on the two refugees sleeping behind the office door only feet away.

That would only piss them both off, Nigel knew. And undirected anger was a hell of a drain on the resources.

"No word, yet. Lydia's starting to get antsy, though, so I've asked my sister-in-law to—Whoa." Jake dropped a hand to the desk, his brow furrowed deeply. "Did you feel that?"

"Another quake?" Nigel stood, but like Jake, he braced both palms on the desk. Nothing moved. Just the usual vibrations of heavy feet tromping through five stories of police station chaos.

Jake frowned. "I'd swear I—"

The light in the police station dimmed slowly. As if a storm front had rolled in beneath Seattle's typical gray clouds. The gray ambience of Seattle's typical daylight turned over the soul-sucking fluorescence of the office lights.

"Holy shit!" Waters snapped a blind back, suddenly pale. "Guys . . . ?"

Nigel circled the desk, hard on Jake's heels as the officer sprinted to the window. Jake pulled the blinds up, the vinyl clattering loudly as the shade rose.

Seattle filled the frame, much as it always did, save for a

little extra wear and tear. As it had been for the past few hours, bumper-to-bumper traffic filled the streets; frightened people hurrying to get out of a city falling apart around them.

The news had promised no more quakes.

They hadn't said anything about the early night.

"What the hell?" Jake breathed.

Nigel watched the thick, lightless bank of clouds roll over the visible skyline. He'd seen it before. Once, when Maylene had faked being sick and he'd let her stay home on his day off. She'd watched a show, some entertainment science. It was about . . . *Oh, shit.*

Even as he opened his mouth, the building shuddered. "Ash," he said, shocked. "That's an ash cloud."

"Quake!" Waters yelled at the same time. The furniture shimmied in place, and Nigel grunted as he turned and slammed thigh-first into the corner of a desk that hadn't been there moments before. The walls swayed, lamps and computer monitors crashed to the floor.

"Get to reinforced positions," someone shouted.

Jake grabbed Nigel's arm as a vicious tremor sent him staggering into a fold-out cubicle. "Get—"

"I'm on it!" Nigel pushed through the room, feeling as if he were forcing each step through knee-high sand. "Katya?"

Cords snapped around him. Light fixtures crashed to the ground, sparks popping. "Evacuate!" someone screamed. "We gotta get out!"

The office door slammed open. Katya staggered out, her hair sleep-tousled and her eyes wild over Junie's head. The girl clung to her, lurching as the floor pitched beneath them.

"Nigel!" Katya held Junie tightly, her eyes pinched with the effort he could clearly see she was exerting to stay calm and upright. "What's happening?"

"Ash cloud. We need to get you out."

"Ash?"

He didn't give her any time to look, grabbing her arm and wrenching her towards the doors. God only knew what was happening, but it wasn't over. Not by a long shot. "Open the doors!"

Stacey slammed at them. "It's stuck," she said, her voice pitched too high. But she worked at the handle, ramming her thin shoulder against it. "Help?"

Nigel wrapped a supporting arm around Katya and Junie as the building rattled violently. "Jake?"

"Here, sir." Jake surged past him, throwing his weight against the doors. Waters joined him, his shoulder working the bent panels. They slammed open.

Waters caught the dark-haired woman around the waist. "You okay, Stace?"

She flashed him a tight little smile. "Great," she said through her teeth. Screams filled the stairway, echoed up to them in a wild cacophony. Even as they crossed the threshold, the hallway creaked and groaned. The stairs rattled, metal and cement tearing free in jagged panels.

Jake leaped back, hauling a screaming Stacey with him. They bowled into Waters and Nigel, sent Katya staggering back into the department doors. She grunted, wincing.

"Christ," Jake breathed as old cement filled the air like the ash looming outside.

Nigel was desperately aware of Junie's small hands at his

waist. He met Katya's eyes over the small group. "Are you okay?"

She nodded, her face pale.

"Ferris!" McClintock's voice cracked like a whip.

Nigel looked up the swaying stairwell. "Chief, we gotta—"

"There's a chopper on the roof," she cut in. "Let's go."

"Chief?" Jake frowned. "Are you bleeding?"

For the first time, Nigel noticed the dark smear of blood on the woman's face. "Shannon!"

She shook her head, mouth tight. "Haul ass, people."

Even as she ducked from view, the stairs groaned again. Nigel grabbed Stacey, pushed her to the front of the group. "Take her," he said, thrusting Junie into her arms.

"Katya," Junie wailed, reaching for her.

Katya struggled to maintain her footing, clutching the door frame for support. She cried out a flurry of Russian.

His grasp wasn't that great under duress. He caught *go* and *sweetheart* and roared, *"Move it."*

They surged up the stairs, in pairs and singles, clinging to the railing as the supports creaked and swayed. Junie clung to Stacey's hands, sobbing in fear, Jake right behind them to lend a hand as he could.

Nigel grabbed Katya as she flailed, her feet thrown out from under her by a particularly violent surge. "What is happening?" she gasped.

He didn't dare take the time to answer. His fingers tight at her elbow, he half-threw her up the stairwell as Waters followed, swearing.

Two flights of stairs suddenly seemed like an eternity. The whole structure heaved, screaming, cracking. Cement steps fell apart, practically beneath them. Finally, Stacey pushed through the rooftop door, pulled Junie out of the way. Jake ran toward the chopper with the chief at his side. She held her head, blood seeping through her fingers.

Nigel let Katya dash through the door, turning to help Waters. He thrust out a hand. "Move it, Andy!"

The stairwell creaked and echoed, dragged a screaming crescendo across his ears. Caught halfway down the staircase, the grizzled detective met Nigel's wild eyes through gray, dust-smeared resignation.

The moment dragged to a standstill.

For one, eternally long second, Nigel held out his hand.

Waters reached for it, his face red. His teeth bared as he strained to clear the steps.

Not fast enough.

With the support beams broken, the final hinges at the top of the stairwell wrenched free. Nigel yelled; Waters dropped his hand as grit and metal rained around them. He shook his head, gripping the swaying railing, and his lips moved.

A prayer. A curse. Hell, Nigel didn't know.

Whatever it was, it was still on his lips as the stairs collapsed beneath him. Anger slammed through him as Waters's gray head vanished in a cloud of crumbled cement and dust.

It all crunched five stories below. Brick and bone and one of the finest badges Nigel had ever known.

He dropped to his knees as if he'd be able to pluck the detective from the ruins, tears aching behind his gritty, burning eyes.

"Ferris, let's go!" The chief yelled. "That's an *order,* detective."

He staggered to his feet. Flailed as the crumbling ledge behind him cracked a warning. With monumental effort, he sprinted onto the roof, mentally saying good-bye to the man who'd taught him what it meant to be a damn fine detective in an unforgiving department.

He met Katya's gaze as he ducked low, approaching the small group beneath the chopper's rotating wings. She touched his arm. "Did he—?"

He shook his head. "How many seats?" he asked roughly, pitching his voice over the *whup, whup, whup* of the whirling rotors.

"With the pilot?" The chief nodded shakily to the man bent over the console, earphones firmly over his head. "Four."

Clumps of gray floated on the air, stirred into a miniature blizzard. Jake's cheek was smeared with black and gray, and the roof was filling with it.

They were running out of time.

And space.

Nigel met Jake's tense gaze and nodded. He'd be the bad guy. With his heart in his throat and the building shuddering beneath them, he ordered, "Katya, Junie, get in the chopper. She can sit on your lap."

"But I—"

He spoke over her, grimly closing his ears—his traitorous heart—to her arguments. "Stacey, you get the second seat. Chief, take the last one, get medical help as fast as you can."

Jake handed Stacey into the helicopter, his features rigid. Her eyes filled with tears. "But what about you?" she demanded. "There's one more seat!"

Nigel said nothing, avoiding Katya's stare.

Jake shook his head. "The bird won't take all the weight. The last seat's for my girls," he said. "Go get them for me. Tell my wife—" His voice cracked. "Tell her I love her."

Katya handed Junie up beside him. "Get in the helicopter, Officer Leigh."

Nigel stiffened. "Katya, don't—"

The building swayed dangerously. The helicopter skidded, metal skids screaming against the cement roof. The pilot swore. "We gotta go!" he roared. The ash floated down like a cotton blizzard, gummy as it gathered the moisture from Seattle's sky.

"You have a baby to take care of," Katya yelled. Her finger slammed into Jake's chest. "Go take care of them."

The chief stepped back, her face pale beneath the blood, but set. "I'll be less weight," she said flatly. "Jake and his family is a full load."

"Goddamn it!" Nigel grabbed Katya's shoulder. "Get in the fucking cabin," he snarled. "I'm a police officer. I have to stay. You don't!"

"Ten seconds!" the pilot yelled.

"Get in the cabin, Jake," McClintock ordered. She grabbed a pipe for support, wiping a mask of ash from her eyes. "That's an order!"

Stacey clung to Junie, who struggled wildly.

"Katya," the girl sobbed. "Katya!"

"Ya vas lyublyu," Katya called. Tears slid down her cheeks, leaving blackened streaks behind. "Go, get out. Take care of her!"

"Katya!"

Jake look backed at Nigel. His mouth opened.

Nigel caught Katya as she stumbled, flattened a hand over her head to keep her from standing too close to the whirling rotors, and held her protectively. "You idiot," he roared.

"We're leaving!" the pilot said, flipping switches. The engine revved, swirling ash and grit in a thick cloud.

Junie sobbed wildly, and with a last, desperate shake of his head, Jake flung himself into the cabin. Stacey caught his sleeve with one hand as the skids lifted off the swaying roof.

Nigel watched Jake struggle to his knees as the helicopter rose. The ash-smeared officer reached for Junie, gathering her to his chest.

A damn good father.

Nigel turned away. "We need to get off this roof," he said, forcing himself into the now. Katya changed everything. "Before the damned thing comes down."

Her face pale beneath a fine dusting of ash, Katya pointed to the side. "The fire escape is—"

The rhythmic noise of the helicopter rotors fractured.

McClintock shouted a warning, her grip white on the bent pipe, but it was too late. Nigel whirled, saw the helicopter tilt awkwardly in the air. He could just barely make out the shape of the pilot, reaching up to flip switches. Pull levers. Ash coated the cabin's windows.

Katya clung to his forearms, her eyes huge. Fearful. "What's happening?"

The engine above them sputtered. Nigel stared in shocked stillness as the chopper swung wide. Its engines coughed, revved once. Choked.

Died.

"It's the ash," he realized with dawning horror. The helicopter dropped as if in slow motion, swinging like a pendulum, its tail forcing the machine into a staggered spin.

Katya screamed, wrenching out of his arms. She sprinted, half-lurching, half-throwing herself to the edge of the roof as the helicopter dropped below the roof's edge. "Turn it on!" she sobbed. "Go, go, oh, God—Junie!"

"Katya!" He pitched after her. There was nowhere for that machine to go but down. Straight down, to an already rickety foundation.

There was a terrible crunch; the shriek of metal twisting, compacting, tearing into brick and mortar. Katya grabbed the lip of the roof, and Nigel swore as a dull *boom* tore through the oddly muffled air.

He reached her just as Katya screamed, tears streaming down her cheeks, hands reaching for dead air. He snatched her back from the edge. Cursed again, over and over as a bloom of fire and smoke blossomed from the street below. The station shuddered; different from the earthquake.

A hollow rumble resonated from beneath them, and fire licked over the edge, searing the air. Thick, black, oily smoke roiled into the sky, and Katya screamed and screamed, her grit-smeared features painted wicked orange as Nigel pinned her to the roof.

With an eerie sense of déjà vu, he clenched his jaw as remnants of steel rained around them. Something hard and sharp slammed into his back, rebounded off his thigh. He grunted.

Katya slammed a fist against the roof.

The whole thing shifted.

Chapter Seven

It wasn't over. Nigel raised his head, blinking away the stinging remains of the smoke-thickened air. Katya sobbed beneath him, and the chief clung to her pipe with obvious strain.

But her gaze wasn't on them. Or the edge where the helicopter had just impacted. She stared at her feet. Her lips moved.

The building rumbled again, too sharp to be an earthquake. Too hard.

Too . . . steep.

"It's coming down!"

Nigel leapt to his feet, grabbed Katya and pulled her upright. "We need to get off this roof," he roared. "Chief!"

"Stairs?" she asked.

He shook his head, cursed and reeled as the building banked sharply to the left. His stomach pitched. Katya choked off a shriek as he wrenched her towards the nearest pipe sticking out from a brick foundation. She clung to it.

He tripped over his own feet as the building swayed again. Like a domino teetering on the edge. Back and forth.

Gritting his teeth, he reached for the pipe. Swore, and then swore again as warm fingers grabbed his.

Katya's gaze was too bright in her filthy face. Her mouth set into a grim, dirty line.

"The roof," McClintock called. Years of running a station had groomed her voice to carry. She flung a hand toward the neighboring building. "Catch it on the backswing!"

Nigel followed the line of her finger. His eyes widened, and then narrowed. "There's no way we can jump—"

"Yes, there is!" she cut in deftly. She inched around her pipe, clung to it with both hands behind her. Her eyes pinned on him. "Do it, or die here."

Nigel looked down at Katya, framed in his arms. Her jaw shifted, strong little chin mulish. "I can do it," she said tightly. "What do I do?"

Nigel's chest swelled. She was so Goddamned brave. "The building's swaying hard enough to topple any second," he explained. "In a moment, it's going to swing back around and probably crash into the one beside us."

She nodded, her face pale.

"When that happens, we jump like hell for the next roof and use the momentum to carry us. You got it?"

"Okay."

The roof tilted again, pitching him against Katya. He clung to the pipe as the world tilted on an axis. "Chief?"

"Ready!"

He grabbed Katya's hand, clinging to the cold pipe with the other. She stared at the neighboring building as it lurched closer. "Oh, God," she whispered. "Oh, God, oh, God—"

He locked his jaw. Below them, the sound of the foundation

walls splintering cracked like rapid-fire gunshots. The building slid sideways, tilted and wrenched lopsided as one cornerstone gave out. The roof slanted dangerously. Gravity swept his feet out from under him, wrenched Katya's grip from the pipe.

She screamed, the sound cut off as his grip tightened around hers. His arms snapped tight, wrenched all the way to his shoulder as he grunted a curse, a prayer, and held on with all his might.

They weren't going to make it.

"Go!" he heard over the chaos.

Nigel eyed the angle of the roof, gauged the building slamming towards them too fast. With his heart in his throat, he braced his feet, jerked Katya to the side, and let go.

She screamed. Unable to catch her footing, she staggered; he caught her around the waist, hauled her half under his arm and tried to run the steepening incline.

Gravel and grit skidded beneath his feet. The edge of the roof hit the building beside it, crumbled. Disintegrated. The aftershocks slammed all the way through him; his head, his bones.

His balance.

Halfway down the incline, he stumbled and fell. It was all he could do to curl his body protectively against Katya's as they rolled and scraped and crashed down the rest of the way. Nailing the landing on his back pounded all his remaining breath out of him.

Rock rained down, mixed with slick ash and remnants of the station. He gasped for breath, wheezing, his vision rolling through a darkening landscape.

Katya coughed, groaning.

"Nigel," she managed between gasps. "Nigel?" Her fingers shook against his face.

He forced his eyes open. "Fuck yeah, roof surfing." It rasped.

She sobbed out a laugh. "We have to go. Nigel, we have to—" She sucked in a trembling breath. "The chief? Where's . . . Oh, God."

He forced himself to his elbows, wiping away the grit accumulating on his face. "Shannon?" he demanded. Katya helped him stand and every muscle in his body twanged in retribution. He swallowed it down. Lurched across the rooftop, now slanted from the impact of the taller station house. Rubble skated under him as he pushed his way to the splash of crimson caught between two brick prongs, pipes from two separate rooftops tangled together.

Chief Shannon McClintock was pale and still. The blood smeared across her face was black with ash. Her hands hung beside her.

One was just as black. Too much black, its edges crimson where the ash hadn't clung yet.

He reached for her neck. "Come on, Chief," he breathed. No pulse met his searching fingers.

Her mouth hung slack.

Behind him, Katya's fist curled into the back of his shirt.

He closed his eyes. "Goddamn it!" Violence surged through him; frustration and fear and so much regret, he choked on it.

"I'm so sorry," Katya whispered.

He reached behind him. Took her hand. "We need to go," he said.

Wordless, her face soot- and tear-stained, Katya tugged him away. The building shuddered as the remains of the station house settled. The pipes trapping McClintock's body bent, creaking.

Pain didn't hold a candle to the fury in his soul. Setting his jaw, Nigel firmed his grip on Katya's hand and ran for the fire escape at the other end of the roof.

One police car had survived the madness at least relatively intact. Although covered with a layer of ash, it was more than enough to get them away.

Away from the ruined building. The mass grave site. Junie, her little face so trusting and sad. Jake, soon to welcome a new baby. So many others.

So much destruction.

Katya stared out the grimy window, her head lolling back on the seat. The wipers were barely enough to keep the stuff from sticking to the cracked windshield. It was all Nigel could do to see, much less drive through the wreckage that was Bellevue.

The sky darkened in rapid increments. Katya watched, feeling as if she were trapped in a surreal dream as the last remnants of daylight faded to a night so thick, it was as if it were made of black paint.

"This is Detective Nigel Ferris." His voice cut through the silence, maybe for the thirtieth time. The hundredth. She didn't know. He'd been droning into the handset for an hour, at least. "Seattle P.D. Is there anyone out there?"

Katya rolled her head back to watch him. Her body ached. Her head hurt. Her heart felt as if it were full of red hot knives.

Her arms felt empty without Junie in them.

Nigel hunched over the wheel, as if that would let him

see better through the rain of wet powder. "I repeat, is there anyone out there?" He met her eyes briefly; stark and raw.

She touched his thigh. But what could she say?

I dreamed this would happen.

No, she didn't. She dreamed about all her plans going up in smoke, that's all. *Ved'ma . . .*

Muscles locked under her hand. His grip tightened on the radio, and he brought it to his mouth again as he navigated the car slowly through the wreckage of what had once been an interstate onramp. "This is Detective Nigel Ferris, of the Seattle P.D."

Withdrawing her hand, she closed her eyes.

The radio crackled. "Detective Ferris! Can you read me?"

Katya bolted upright. "Was that—?"

He blew out a hard, anxious breath. "Loud and clear," he said into the device. "Where are you? What's your status?"

"This is Petty Officer First Class Winston Shepherd," came the voice. "United States Coast Guard. There's a small contingency of refugees gathering at the Port Authority station. Can you get to us, detective?"

Nigel's smile was flat, not so much a smile as a razored edge of grim determination. "Yes, sir," he replied. "We'll be there in less than an hour."

"Any women or children with you, detective?"

Katya swallowed a raw sound as he glanced at her. Instead, she raised her chin, even as her throat ached from the effort.

"One," he said. "A woman."

"Copy that. We should have room for both of you."

"Thank you, sir," Nigel replied. "Over and out." He hung

the radio back in place. "Try to get some rest," he told her, but he didn't look at her. "We'll be at the Port Authority before you know it."

"I wonder how many—"

His fingers tightened on the wheel. "Don't," he cut in roughly. She flinched. "Don't think about it."

"What am I supposed to think about?" she asked, knuckling her eyes. "I keep seeing—" Her throat clutched. "She was screaming for me."

He reached over, covered her hand where it braced on the seat. "Talk to me about something else," he said softly. "Where were you born?"

She sucked in a wild breath. "Nigel—"

His grip tightened on hers. Warm. Strong. "Do you have any family?" he persisted.

Katya turned her hand over. Her palm pressed to his, and she watched that muscle in his jaw leap again. The tight one that said he was forcing himself to do something. Not do something. She didn't know. Shaking her head, she clung to his hand and said dully, "No family. Not anymore."

"I'm sorry."

"Don't be." She wiped her gritty forearm across her cheek, already knowing how futile the gesture was. She was coated in ash, gummy with sweat. "My mother was afraid of me."

Nigel frowned. "Of *you*? Why?"

Ved'ma, ved'ma! The word echoed in her dreams, didn't it? Right up there with *whore*. Her smile hurt. "She thought I was a witch."

"No such thing," he scoffed, and she wanted to kiss him.

Except he was wrong. Even if he believed what he said, she was living proof that he was wrong. "They called me *ved'ma*," she continued. "It means—"

"Witch," he said, "I heard Ivan call you that." She shook her head. "No?"

"It's kind of like witch," she said softly, "but it literally means 'one who knows.'"

The smile he bestowed on her was indulgent. Just wry enough that she realized he was trying to defuse what she'd already accepted. Her optimist cop. "And what do you know, Katya?"

She hesitated. Outside the ash fell in soft, dirty flakes, and the windshield wipers strained in the sudden silence. Then, quietly, she admitted, "I dreamed about this."

"What?"

She gestured at the windows. "I started having dreams about the world ending, I thought it was just nerves." She slanted him a glance, but couldn't read anything other than indulgent attention in the dim interior light.

"That's all it was," he said with a shrug. "The mind is weird. How could you possibly know this was coming?"

She sighed. "If I knew that, I'd unlock a giant mystery, wouldn't I?"

He glanced at her, eyebrow slanted. "Is that it? Vague dreams?"

"I can tell if you're lying."

He laughed. "So you can read people—"

"Try me."

He squeezed her hand. "My middle name is Thomas."

Truth. "I could have read that at the station," she pointed out. "Try something I wouldn't know."

His jaw shifted, and he let go of her hand to grab the wheel firmly. "I have a sister."

Lie. Katya shook her head. "No, you don't."

His eyebrows rose. "I hate pineapple."

Truth. Her lips curved. "That's a shame."

"I don't usually like blondes," he continued, his eyes on the blackened street in front of them. The headlights barely carved out a niche in the thick fallout.

She blinked at him. "Truth."

His mouth quirked. "What do you know?"

"Do you believe me?" she demanded.

He didn't look at her. "I don't think it matters."

He believed that. But maybe it did matter. Maybe it mattered to her. Katya looked away, folding her arms over her chest. "If that's all—"

Crack! As if the whole of the world had split in half, the sound fractured through the oddly quiet murmur of ash and rain. She startled, biting back a scream, and jerked around in her seat. "What was that?"

His expression closed, grim as he concentrated on the road. "I don't know."

She reached for the window, hitting the automatic switch. The glass squeaked as it tried to shed the accumulation of ash. When it had lowered enough, she gasped.

A dull, glowing ember hovered on the horizon to the southeast, just barely noticeable through the gritty darkness. She stared. "That's . . . Oh, my God."

"Mount Rainier," Nigel confirmed, his voice bleak. "Welcome to hell on earth."

Shaking, she raised the window again. But she couldn't look away. The red glow flickered through the smeared glass, as if alive.

"Paris," she whispered.

"What?"

"I remember the news." Her throat hurt; too much screaming. Too many swallowed tears. She cleared it. "A storm ripped through it, right? Two years ago."

Nigel said nothing.

"And Florida," she continued raggedly. "A hurricane."

"For God's sake, would people stop bringing up Florida? The damn state's *always* got a hurricane," Nigel said, his gaze hard on the road.

"New Orleans?"

He shook his head. "The city's been a magnet for disaster since someone got the brilliant idea to build below sea level," he said firmly. "It's known for flooding."

She wanted to laugh. It came out as a fractured sob. "God wants to start over," she said, and couldn't keep the edge of hysteria from her own voice. "Did we build too high again? Is this our punishment?"

Warm fingers slid over hers again. Tightened. "God has another thing coming," Nigel promised tersely.

Truth, she thought, and clutched his hand in both of hers.

Maybe he was right. He *believed* what he said, but maybe there was something to it.

Maybe Detective Nigel Ferris could take on God—Mother

Nature, witches, or random chaos, she could take her pick. Maybe he'd take them all on.

It was small comfort.

Her palm to his, Katya leaned back against her seat and tried to sleep.

A dull red glow burned behind her eyes.

Chapter Eight

Ved'ma.

Katya's voice echoed in Nigel's head, punctuated by the soft rhythm of her breath.

The one who knows.

He didn't believe in witches. Sure, there'd been the occasional media sensation over the years, this psychic or that voodoo queen or God only knew what else, but they'd eventually subsided. So-called "witches" were just people who knew how to play the odds.

At least, he'd thought so until now. She'd been right. Every lie he'd given her, she'd been able to tell. And he knew his poker face wasn't that bad.

Was it possible? Did she actually see this coming?

No. Not in a million years. It wasn't *witchcraft* or *voodoo* or whatever occult nonsense people spewed that caused this sort of chaos. It was science. Pure and simple.

The earth hiccupped.

Volcanoes blew.

This was life.

But he couldn't lock out the sound of her voice as she'd asked fearfully about God.

No God would ever allow *this.*

Not to thousands, even millions of Seattle civilians. Innocents. Not to babies like Junie.

Like Maylene.

His knuckles popped around the steering wheel. For the hundredth time, he replayed his daughter's words in his head. *Love you, too.*

She'd said it. Without prompting. Without wheedling. Maylene had told him that she loved him and then Laura had taken her away. Held her hostage because of some stupid point she wanted to make against him.

But maybe it was for the best. His daughter was safe in Bellingham.

Please, let her be safe in Bellingham.

He drove carefully, every muscle throbbing in protest as he navigated the cruiser through the remains of whatever street he was on now. He'd once known Seattle like the back of his hand. Now it sprawled in the false night like a strange junkyard; twisted and broken. He knew he had to aim for the coast. He had that covered.

But there was no telling what they'd find.

Out the window, flickering in and out of view, the fiery glow from Mt. Rainier pulsed. Like a vivid heart in the forced darkness.

Nigel shook his head. "Witches," he muttered. Not likely.

Beside him, Katya stirred.

Even just thinking about her in the seat, filthy and bruised as she was, set his heart racing. He'd almost lost her. Hell, he'd been so eager to put her into that helicopter. He didn't stop to think about the ash cloud, or the intake clogging with it.

It was his fault that Jake would never meet his new baby. If that baby was even alive.

He clenched his teeth, his eyes burning. They'd come this far. He'd be damned if he'd lose Katya, too.

She opened her eyes. They glittered in the dark, a diamond glint of blue. "Nigel."

"We're not there yet," he said quietly. "Relax."

She didn't. Resting one hand on the dash, she leaned forward, her mouth bent in a puzzled frown. "Do you hear that?"

He glanced at her. Noted the haggard lines by her mouth. The exhaustion she shoved aside as if it were nothing. He shook his head. "You were dreaming—"

"Shh." She depressed the window button. It crept down a mere inch and then stuck, its mechanism likely filled with the sooty residue of Rainier's temper. "Damn."

"Katya—" But then Nigel stilled. Instinctively, he depressed the brake, slowing their already frustrating crawl down to a snail's pace.

The sound he'd taken for the ambient noise of ash slushing against city wreckage seemed different somehow. He hunched over the wheel, squinting to see through the dark. The headlights only picked out a wall of floating soot, definitely not the source of the rushing sound around them. "I can't see."

She flattened a palm against her window, pensive. "What's going on?"

"It's okay," he said, responding to the fear in her voice. "We're almost to the port."

She opened her mouth. The rushing sound rose to a heady roar.

His eyes widened. "Katya," he said, and the two syllables sharpened on a harsh warning. She half-turned, but he grabbed her by the back of the neck and pulled her down, half-across the seat. Too fast to be gentle.

Not fast enough.

Water slammed against the passenger side of the car, crashing into the metal and safety glass like an explosion; a fist of cement. The cruiser flipped. Glass crunched as the police lights on top exploded into fragments, metal ground.

Nigel grunted as his seat belt snapped across his chest, thrusting him back into his seat with the rebound. He heard Katya's scream, but she wasn't in his grip anymore. The car flipped again, and again. Rolling and turning with every pounding thrust of the flood as it swept over them.

End over end; the world turned and righted and turned until he didn't know which side was up. His stomach pitched and yawned, his chest aching from the pressure of his seat belt.

Pain seared through his head as the car slammed against something.

Swearing, still seeing stars, he fumbled his seat belt loose. It gave way, and he reached out in the near-perfect darkness.

He found gritty, cold skin. "Katya!"

Hands caught his, wet but strong. "I'm here," she managed, her voice tight.

There wasn't any time for relief.

"We need to get out before the water in here traps us in,"

he explained quickly. He fumbled for his door latch. "As soon as I open this—"

"I get it." Her hands found the back of his shirt. Held tight. "Ready."

He grunted. His options were slim. Either die in a watery tomb, or risk dying out there of exposure, hypothermia, or worse.

He swallowed hard. "One . . ."She sucked in a hard, painful breath.

"Two."

He closed his eyes. *Please . . .*

"Three!" He rammed the door with his shoulder as he pulled the latch. The pressure in the car tightened, as if a vacuum sucked on the door, resisted his effort. He strained, muscles popping, strained with everything he had.

All at once, it whooshed open. Nigel caught the door frame in one hand as water sluiced through the sudden opening. He grabbed Katya with the other, helped her out, and held her to the rim as she grabbed the hood.

She gasped. "We're moving!"

He'd been afraid of that.

Gritting his teeth, he wrenched himself out of the interior. The current flowed over his battered body, soaking him to the bone in seconds. "Up," he rasped.

She grabbed the hood, stretched as high as she could and tried to climb to the somewhat drier territory on top of the busted cruiser. Nigel forced himself up beside her, collapsing to his hands and knees as the car rocked dangerously.

Katya clung to him, panting.

He didn't know where they were anymore. He didn't know

how fast they were moving; hell, he didn't even know what fucking side of town they were on.

Gasping for breath, he clung to the roof edge with one hand and tucked an arm around Katya.

She gasped, her body stiffening.

"Oh, shit," he said tightly, and caught her by the shoulders instead. "Are you hurt?"

Her lips gleamed faintly as they curved up in the dark. Wry. Apologetic. "My side hurts." Her voice was a whisper.

"Hurts how?"

"Burning." She huddled against his side, tucking herself under his arm as if he'd somehow be able to protect her. Fuck, he couldn't.

Burying his face in her soaking hair, he muttered, "Bruised ribs, maybe. Cracked. Christ, Katya."

She eased out a shaking, sodden sound of exhaustion. A sigh; a laugh. He didn't know.

As his eyes adjusted, he picked out details as they passed. Sparking cords to the right, some remnant of an electrical supply. Ruined, half-buried tenements on the left.

She sagged against him, her fingers tight at his waist. He looked down, saw the vague outline of her profile as she stared towards the southeast. Mt. Rainier flickered and danced; a vibrant orange knot smoldering in the dark.

"It's . . ." She took a deep breath; he felt her body recoil as it hurt. "It's weirdly beautiful, isn't it?"

Nigel closed his eyes. He pressed his lips to her hair, inhaling the fragrance of ash, woman, and the unique scent of salt.

The fragrance of ocean.

It didn't matter where they were now. They'd never get to

Petty Officer First Class Winston Shepherd. They'd never find the Port Authority.

The flood had come from Puget Sound.

The port was gone.

She dozed awkwardly in his embrace. Nigel shivered, tightening his arms around her, trying to channel every ounce of warmth he had left into her body.

He'd taken his flannel off, draping it over them. It filtered the worst of the ash out, but he had to shake it more and more often. The cloud was thickening.

She stirred now and again. But because he couldn't help himself, he checked her pulse as often as he could.

Every few seconds, it felt like.

Katya shivered. "Nigel?"

He rested his cheek against her hair. The car bumped gently, but he resisted the urge to look. He was desperately afraid it'd be another corpse.

He'd seen a few. Pale and ghostly beneath the water.

He closed his eyes. "What, sweetheart?"

There was a pause. Then, so softly he almost missed it, she asked, "Did you wonder why I . . . Did you want to know why I was there? In that place?"

He smiled. "Because you're a Good fucking Samaritan."

She raised her head. Muttered a hard word of pain and sank back into his embrace. He cradled her as closely as he dared, one hand spread across her rib as if he could protect it by his touch alone.

Oh, how he wished.

"Yes," he answered, to give her something else to think about. "Why don't you tell me?"

She was silent for a moment. He tipped the flannel slightly. Ash slid to the damp car roof with a whisper-soft sound.

"We were going to escape, you know," she murmured. "We had it all planned out. I went to the police to ask for help."

He was too exhausted to be angry. Still, the thought bit hard.

"They said no," she said, her voice thready with pain. She leaned back against his chest, and he looked down to see her eyes closed. Her mouth curved down, pinched with effort.

"I'm sorry," he murmured.

"I guess I . . . hoped you'd help me. When I saw you, when you picked me, I thought maybe you'd come to help."

"I'm a bastard," Nigel said tightly.

"No." She shook her head. "No, you're not." The car thudded. She gasped.

Nigel smoothed back her hair, gritting his teeth to keep them from chattering. "It's all right."

But it wasn't. With dismay, he realized that tears slipped from beneath her lashes. She bit her lip, clutching his arm as if afraid he'd let her go.

He wouldn't. "It's all right," he said again, soft as he could. "Why did you go back to the house? You were out, you could have run."

"I couldn't leave them," she admitted, turning her face into his chest. He cradled her cheek, bending his head over hers. "All those girls . . . All those *men*. I couldn't leave them there. And now . . . now they're probably all dead anyway, aren't they?"

Ah. Now he got it. Nigel held her as she cried, staring into the darkness in silence. What could he say? He knew survivor's guilt.

As she sank again into a broken sleep, all he could do was thank God that she was here with him.

Not helpful.

The car shuddered again. Silence stretched across minutes, maybe hours.

He dozed fitfully.

Without warning, the car jarred hard. The impact knocked him backward. Katya shrieked awake, jolted out of his arms, and he barely managed to catch himself on the edge of the hood.

Katya grabbed her side, her eyes wild. "Nigel?"

He looked down. Saw mud, rubble.

And a corpse. Another. Bloated, pallid. Scraped raw.

Fury lanced through him. "No," he gritted out. The waters had receded, sucked back into the ocean after the tidal wave had run its course, but he'd be damned if this was it for them.

"No?"

He rolled off the car, landed awkwardly in ankle-deep mud. "Come here." When she scooted near enough, he pulled her into his exhausted arms. His chest kicked as she looped her arms around his check. "Stay with me," he ordered hoarsely. "I don't care how cold you get, how bad it hurts, you stay with me, you understand?"

She leaned her head against his shoulder, but he felt her nod.

Slowly, mustering every ounce of energy he had left, he

forced one foot through the mud. Then the next. One more. The other.

Step by step. Block by ruined city block. Past the skeletons of ruined buildings, past the corpses piled by the destructive, unfeeling currents.

He didn't know how long they walked. Tremors rippled through the earth beneath his feet, but as long as he could stay upright, he walked.

Katya clung to him, too spent to even shake.

He wouldn't die here. He wouldn't let her die here, either. She hadn't gone through years of hell to lose it here.

He hadn't gone through everything he had to lose her to it.

Another vicious tremor rolled underfoot, and he paused, half-collapsing against a fractured telephone pole. Panting for breath, his legs and back screaming, he briefly rested his head against the sodden wood.

Katya cracked open a crusted, ash-smudged eye. "Do you . . . Do you hear that?

He stiffened, adrenaline forcing a painful stream through his veins. "Not again," he rasped.

"No. No, it's—"

His head snapped up. "An engine!" He scoured the horizon, for all he couldn't see much more than a few feet. Lights. Just give him lights. Search lights, tail lights. Was it an airplane?

No, not in the ash field.

A car?

Suddenly, a horn blasted across his senses, tearing jagged furrows through his control. He pushed away from the pole, letting Katya slide down his body. Her feet touched the ground, and she half-pushed, half-pulled him into the road. Or what he hoped was the road. "Oh, God," she said hoarsely. "Please. Please!"

He squinted, shading his eyes with a filthy hand. Was it his imagination?

No. "Lights," he said. And then, louder, "Katya, lights!" With an arm around her shoulders, he waved wildly in the spark's direction. "Help," he shouted. "Hey! Over here!"

"They're turning." Tears thick in her voice, Katya sagged against him.

He looked down at her. Five feet and two inches of grim fucking determination covered head to toe in grime and soot, with her hair colored the same dingy gray as he was sure his was.

As a massive truck rumbled into view, he caught her face between his palms and said fiercely, "I love you, woman."

Her eyes widened.

He bent and seized her mouth in a celebratory kiss. As her hand slid around the back of his head, he bent and swept her once more into his arms. Air brakes screeched. "Hey!" he heard, and lifted his head to find a grimy, bespectacled man leaning out of the window.

He waved. "Coming, then?"

Nigel looked down at the woman in his arms, her eyes filled with pain. But her mouth curved up. "Let's go," she whispered.

He forged through the ankle-deep sludge. The truck was large, some type of long-distance trailer attached to the cab. The man beckoned him back, and he heard the creak of a ramp being lowered.

"Thank you," he said to the driver. "You have no idea."

"I do," the man said. "There's help back there, go on."

As he rounded the trailer, a woman met him at the top of the ramp. She was young, maybe early to mid-twenties, with high cheekbones and ash-streaked red hair woven into a messy braid. Her brown eyes were serious as she beckoned them up. "Here, bring her," she said. Her voice was husky, her tone authoritative.

Katya held his shirt in one hand as he climbed the ramp.

She gasped.

The trailer was filled with people.

They sat huddled in groups, some wearing scrubs. Others, like him, wore whatever they'd been caught in and enough grime to mask any detail of color.

The woman's fingers slipped under his elbow and he started. "In," she ordered. "Is your lady hurt?"

"Ribs," he said automatically. "I think they're bruised."

She smiled from underneath a fringe of ash-tipped red hair. "It's okay. We're going to get everyone out. Take her that way." She pointed to a small knot of exhausted looking women. "Erin?"

One, a blonde sporting a thick scab across her cheek and dirty nursing scrubs, looked up. Upon seeing Katya in Nigel's arms, she straightened. "Bring her."

He stepped over hands and legs and made his excuses. Faces blurred. So many. At least thirty crammed into the trailer. Many wearing hospital clothes. He saw two IVs, their bags affixed to the trailer rafters.

As he set Katya down on the floor, the back of his neck prickled. He turned, met the woman's warm brown eyes. She tucked a shoulder-length braid behind her as she bent to place a wad of clothing under Katya's head. "She'll be okay," she said, though he hadn't asked.

The window between trailer and cap cracked open. "Mattie?"

She didn't turn. "We're set, Laurence. Go."

The window snicked shut.

Erin worked quickly, raising Katya's shirt and feeling around the livid bruise climbing from hip to breast.

"How bad is it out there?" he asked, his eyes on Katya.

The woman called Mattie crouched as the truck lurched into motion. Everyone swayed, holding the walls, the window frames build into the sides, and each other.

The shadows outside passed in a blur.

"It's bad," she said. "But we're going to get everyone to a safe place."

Nigel looked down at his hands, clasped tightly.

Mattie reached over, touched his shoulder. "Your lady will be fine. She's strong."

His throat worked. No sound came. Then, slowly, raggedly, he asked, "Bellingham. Is it—?" His voice betrayed him. It broke as he read the truth in her steady regard.

In her sympathy.

"I'm sorry," she told him, shaking her head. "Mount Baker erupted."

Erin looked up from the bandages she wrapped around Katya's ribs. "Not so much erupted as blew out," she told him. "Near as we can tell, there was a sudden flurry of volcanic activity in the Ring of Fire. It touched off even the dormant ones. The shockwave obliterated Bell—"

He rose to his feet so fast, he had to slam a hand against

the window for balance. Refugees startled awake around him.

"Erin really." Mattie frowned at her, disapproval clear in her voice.

She winced. "Sorry, Dr. Lauderdale."

Nigel barely heard. Shaking his head, over and over, he picked his way through a sea of faceless refugees. Not that he could go anywhere.

There was nowhere to go.

His world had become a trailer filled with strangers.

"May Day," he whispered as he gripped the edge of a window. He stared out into it, saw only ash and the glowing ember of hell inside it.

Love you, too, Dad.

The strangers said nothing as tears slid from his gritty eyes.

Chapter Nine

The trailer was quiet. Now and then, a child's voice rose on a sob or a question, to be hushed by whatever exhausted adult was nearby.

Exhaustion filled her to the bone. Wrapped so tightly she could barely breathe, Katya remained silent while she watched Nigel in the dim interior. He stared out of the dingy window and didn't bother wiping away his tears.

Tears for his city?

For someone else?

She'd been so selfish. While she had been so focused on herself, she'd never bothered to ask him what—who—he'd lost in the cataclysm.

The truck shook, jarring everyone inside as another earthquake tore through the bedrock. Mattie linked hands with some of the more frightened children. "It's all right," she soothed.

They clung to her as if they knew her. Children from the hospital? Was she a doctor?

A doctor who'd saved those she could.

Katya got carefully to her feet. Mindful of the crowded conditions, she worked her way through the tangled knot of people until she could slip her fingers into the window frame beside Nigel's for balance.

"Nig—"

He didn't let her get a word out. Silently, he turned, caught her in one arm and crushed her to him in a hug that stole the last of the breath from her body.

What could she do? As he buried his face in her hair, she held onto him. As tightly as if he'd fade, cease to exist if she didn't. As if she could tell him without speaking how much he meant to her.

He whispered something ragged against her hair.

The terrible, shattering *crack* of thunder came again. The glow beyond the ash flared wildly, suddenly lighting the sooty sky to a muddy orange.

They lurched against the wall as the truck swayed. Screams punctuated the creak and echo of hands and bodies hitting the walls, the floors.

Mattie grabbed the nearest children and herded them against the wall. "Hold on," she ordered. "Laurence!"

The window cracked open. "Earthquake," came the man's voice, locked down with obvious tension. Obvious control. "It's a big one, so hang on tight."

Nigel's arms folded her closer. Katya raised on her tiptoes, trusting in his greater strength, and pressed her lips to the hollow of his throat. It was as far as she could reach.

He rasped something that could have been a laugh.

The truck lurched, trembling violently as Laurence tried to stabilize it. Tucking Katya between his body and the wall,

Nigel grabbed the window frame again. His hips locked her in place.

His arms strained on either side of her body, protective and strong.

Leaning against his chest, she watched as Mt. Rainier spewed and frothed. The trailer jostled wildly, bucking as if it would break in two.

Nigel's stance, military-strong, braced as he held her. "Hell on earth," he murmured over her head.

He didn't have to say more. As one, as if by some unspoken order, the refugees clung to each other and silently watched as the southern edge of Seattle's skyline crumbled.

Katya loosely wrapped her fingers around Nigel's wrists, her thumbs squarely on his steady, rapid pulse, and took a deep, aching breath. *I love you, too,* she thought. Truth.

But now wasn't the time.

Maybe once they were safe, she could tell him.

Maybe, just maybe, it'd be enough to soothe some of the haunted look from his eyes.

The horizon spat orange fire.

"Hang on tight," Mattie ordered. "We're not out yet."

Nigel's arm tucked around Katya's ribs, and she took as deep a breath as the bandages would allow. Screw timing. *"Ya vas lyublyu,"* she whispered.

He looked down at her. "I know. God, I hope it's enough."

It had to be. Love was all they had to give, now.

The truck engine roared as Laurence stomped on the gas.

Epilogue

The medical truck carrying thirty-two refugees eventually made it out of the Pacific Northwest, traveled south into California, and found—and lost—more souls along the way. As the aftershocks faded into the occasional tremor behind them, the refugees split into groups of shared ideology.

The most vocal of these were those desperately searching for someone to blame.

Mattie and Laurence Lauderdale kept their patients close, while a band of more militant refugees became one of a handful of marauders determined to survive at all costs. Even if it meant leaving others to die.

Katya and Nigel left with a small group of hopeful idealists, pioneers determined to make it in this new world. Somewhere in the south of the devastated country, they found and fell in love with a small parcel of land by the ocean and developed a commune. Although they would never know it, Katya's first child became the first baby born after the cataclysm.

Like her mother, she was a witch.

But witches weren't welcome in America anymore.

It would be three years before the extent of the damage

could be processed, but the repercussions began almost immediately. Terrified and eager for an answer, encouraged by a religious sect that had somehow survived the disaster intact, the country saw a scapegoat in the men and women deemed too "different" to be human—and enacted the worst witch hunts in humanity's bloody history.

It would be years before humanity finally managed to find some footing amid the rubble, but those years would remain a gory wound in the memories of all who experienced them. Governments were scrapped, many surviving leaders fed to the witch fires. New leaders were shaped into shadow councils bent on serving tyrants or pale imitations of the republics they used to be.

In America, the federal government lost ground to state leaders, and isolationism increased as only the most urban metropolitan areas were rebuilt. Survivors flocked to these bastions of safety, to find refuge behind newly built city walls.

The Holy Order of St. Dominic rose as the undisputed king of the new era, and at their side the witch hunting mission became a weapon of mass annihilation.

Millions died, in Seattle and across the world. But at least a third fell to the fires of zealotry.

Later, as the survivors organized, they would come to understand that the San Andreas Fault had fractured. Every sister fault along the massive chasm's trajectory cracked wide, as far north as the ruins of Vancouver and nearly as far south as Mexico, which had lost half its land mass beneath the sea. South America was cut off, and all contact eventually lost.

Most of Seattle slid into the new fault, bringing an end to any hope of search and rescue operations. They called the chasm the Sea Trench, as tons of water from the Puget Sound roared through it.

New York, Chicago, Detroit, even farther to England, Germany, Italy, Japan. New Zealand was gone, washed clean by tsunamis created by tectonic shifts so massive that it split the island in two.

Humanity had only just barely survived the worst years of its millennial history, and they were sure that witches were to blame—hellish creatures spawned of Satan and whose very presence, whose very tolerance among God's children, had caused Him to punish the whole world.

Millennia ago, it had been a flood. This was no different.

And while the fanaticism ran hot and bloody, scientists gathered data. Measured it, calculated it, argued over and filed it. They delivered reports to their respective countries, many too splintered to have the resources to care, and those files were lost, misplaced, or burned—with the brilliant mind who delivered it—as heresy.

Science had no place in the Holy Order's domination.

It would be over fifty years before those files would come to light. Each culminating in a single warning:

The cataclysm will come again.

About the Author

Born from the genetic mash-up of lesser royalty, storytellers, wanderers and dreamers, Karina Cooper couldn't help but be a writer. After writing happily ever afters for all of her friends, she eventually grew up (kind of) and fell in love with paranormal romance. Because, really, who doesn't love hot men and a happy ending?

When she isn't writing about things that go bump in the night, Karina designs Steampunk and neo-Victorian couture for gentlemen hobbyists and ladies of questionable reputation. She lives in the beautiful Pacific Northwest with a husband, four cats, one rabbit, the fantasy of a dog and a passel of adopted gamer geeks. She adores hearing from readers, so grab a cup of tea and visit www.karinacooper.com.

Coming Soon from Karina Cooper

Blood of the Wicked

June 2011

Lure of the Wicked

July 2011

Keep reading for a
Sneak peak at
Karina Cooper's first novel
In her Dark Mission series

Blood of the Wicked

Coming June 2011
From Avon Books

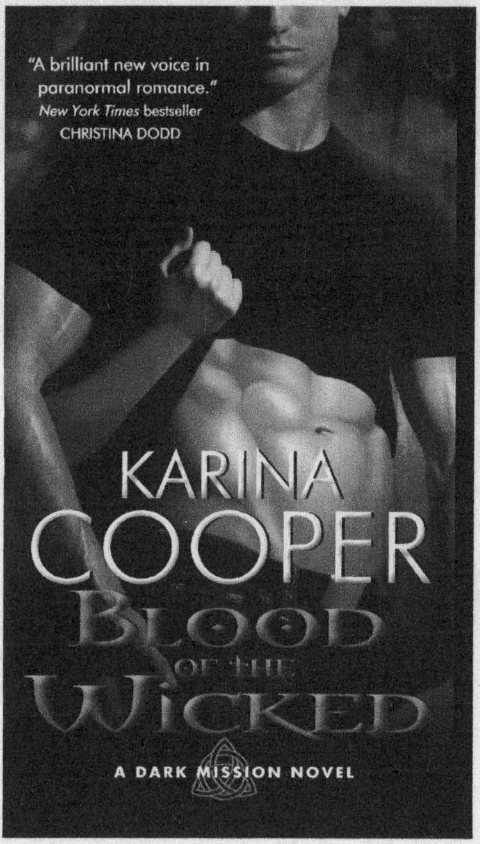
"A brilliant new voice in paranormal romance."
New York Times bestseller
CHRISTINA DODD
KARINA
COOPER
BLOOD
OF THE
WICKED
A DARK MISSION NOVEL

Chapter One

Operation Echo Location reeked.

Silas Smith knew bullshit when he smelled it. Sure, it smelled a lot like sweat and cigarette smoke and desperation, but it was pure bullshit. Shoved into a manila envelope and jammed down his throat.

Fuck, his head hurt. The overloud electronic crap they called music at the Pussycat Perch began its skull-wrecking vendetta the instant he stepped through the door. The pain fed off the industrial bass rocking the foundations of the converted warehouse, played counter to the painful throb of his left knee. Between light, sound, pain, and the shitty mood he'd been nursing since he'd returned to the damned city, it was all he could do to figure out where the hell anything was around him.

Silas blinked in the scattered flash of multicolored beams of light. Every breath burned, smoke and humid energy sliding over his tongue. Dancers filled the floor to capacity, writhing in a sea of light and limbs and gleaming, sweaty skin. Gyrating, mostly naked women wrapped around bolted poles at three stages, and the cacophony skewered through his brain, pissing him off even more than when he'd walked in.

Finding anyone in this mess was going to be a complete pain in the ass. As with every joint like it, the Perch had built its success on too-loud music, too many people, too much skin.

Sex, drugs, and debts too deep to ever climb out of. He'd see it here in the too-bright eyes of the avid voyeurs and the dead, doll-like stares of the women who danced for them.

So he'd find Jessica Leigh and get the hell out again. Where the fuck was the bar?

It took him several minutes to find it, scarred wood countertops hidden behind a sea of demanding customers. It took longer to force his way through the oversexed crowd. Dancers thrashed around him, drunks staggered by, and he'd made it halfway through the mess before white-hot static shorted his brain on a crackled snap of pain.

Instinctively he caught the woman who'd slammed into him, elbow to gut and knee to knee, barely cognizant of her slurred apology. He pushed past her, cursing, forging through the masses as he fumbled in his pocket for the aspirin he kept close.

The chaos around the bar was an ocean of calm compared to the death trap of a dance floor. He grabbed the edge of the wooden bar to stake his claim to a foot-wide piece of real estate, even as he popped the painkillers into his mouth dry.

"What'll it be?"

Silas turned at the husky half shout near his ear, caught an eyeful of red velvet and smooth, bare skin. He swallowed the bitter pills on pure reflex.

She was sex wrapped up in gold ribbon.

Tight, trim curves smoothed out a wine-dark corset strapped with gold. The overhead lights cast radiant colors over her bare arms and shoulders, gleamed over her wavy tousle of black hair. Her wide mouth curved up at one corner, painted bloody crimson and guaranteed to make a man like him take notice.

He did. So did his dick. Contrary to every vicious reminder of how much he hated strip joints, he was suddenly, viscerally aware of the rhythmic bass thudding inside his chest. And his jeans.

"I said," she repeated, throaty amusement coloring the half-shouted words, "what'll it be?"

Sweat and sex and your mouth on my—

Jesus Christ, that wasn't right. He hadn't come out here to troll for ass. Silas reached into his inner coat pocket. "Looking for someone."

"Sorry, they're not here." Bright. Smooth.

Silas studied her light brown eyes. Whiskey eyes, he thought, and frowned. "How do you know who I'm looking for?"

"Doesn't matter." She braced slim arms on the bar top, giving him a tantalizing view of the cinched-up swell of her small breasts. Notched, grimy bills peeked out from beneath her bodice, startlingly dirty against the clean shine of her skin.

He jerked his gaze back up to her face. "I need—"

"They aren't here," she repeated, firmer this time. Velvet and steel. "So what do you drink?"

Lust warred with annoyance. Pure frustration. So the Perch was one of those places. Hell, and why not? Silas settled for a nod. "Beer."

He peeled a few small bills from the clip in his inner jacket pocket. It gave him plenty of time to admire the taut curve of her ass under barely-there gold shorts as she bent over the back counter, retrieved an unlabeled brown bottle. Glass hit the bar with a thump, and her fingers closed over the money.

He held on just a second too long. Just long enough to make his own point.

Her gaze dropped to his hand, to the money and the wooden beads strung on a leather cord around his wrist. The black tattoo half concealed under the hem of his sleeve. "Nice ink." She plucked the bills from his loosened grasp. "Holler if you want another."

With a whirl of gold ribbon and practiced rhythm, she turned and strode back down the bar. Silas watched her go, unable to help himself as his gaze raked over her long bare legs.

Tempting. And because it was, she was interesting. He didn't do strippers. And, he reminded himself, shifting on the stool, he had work to do. His fingers itched to pull out the photo from his inner pocket, to refocus. From the moment he'd laid eyes on the picture, Jessica Leigh's laughing, youthful face had captured him. Branded itself on his brain. She was radiant, caught in a moment of complete candid delight. Wholesome. Fragile.

Nothing like the cunning, son of a bitch witch in the picture with her.

So here he was, because he'd gotten a call from a ghost he'd thought he'd long since left behind with this damned city and didn't know how to say no.

Find her. Land her. Easy, right?

He waited with a raw impatience that ate at his already fraying control. By the time an hour crawled by, he'd finished his beer and the pain in his knee had mellowed to a dull ache.

He was four aspirin down and seven come-ons up, and annoyed as hell when the latest in a string of stage-light strippers turned out to be bleached blond and *not* Jessica Leigh.

He set the empty bottle on the counter, turned to wave the bartender over, and found her tucked back by the employee hatch. One hand curved around the hinged slat of wood, holding it up while she withdrew a small wad of bills from her cleavage.

The short blond in front of her took it, nodded, and Silas's pulse spiked hard as adrenaline surged through his system. The riot of noise in the club amplified through his skull as he half stood, ready to move. Get her, get the hell out. She turned, and Silas blew out a disappointed breath.

Damn it. Just another blond in a fake leather halter, and one hell of a rack to frame in it.

He was getting tired of this undercover shit. He sat back down, reached for his drink. Remembered it was empty and jammed his elbows on top of the counter instead. Fuck. This. Job. He wasn't a subtle investigation kind of guy. More got done at the business end of the revolver tucked beneath his jacket, but he'd let himself get suckered into this one.

Damn Naomi West for finding him.

He glanced over when the hatch slammed closed. The long-legged bartender locked it in place and sauntered across the floor. Silas watched her because, hell, her hips swayed like she knew what five inches of gold spiked heel did to a man.

Sharply sweet floral perfume speared through his nose as the new blond with the impressive boob job snagged his empty bottle and tossed it into a bin behind her. Glass shattered. "Another one, sugar?"

"No, thanks."

She followed his gaze, grinning a full-lipped, catlike grin. "Your favorite? She's hot enough, I guess. I told her she'd make better tips if she stayed blond, men love it. Does she listen to me? Hell, no. I've only been in this business for three years, you know? I make damn good money."

Only half listening, Silas grimaced, shifting his leg to ease the pain. Yeah, the brunette was hot, but she wasn't what he needed. Jessica wasn't here. He'd come back tomorrow, and the next night. See if she showed up, or if the intel had been wrong after all.

He paused. Frowned. *She'd make better tips if she stayed blond.*

Light brown eyes. Full mouth. Wide cheekbones— *Hell.* Jessica.

Silas shot to his feet in time to watch the employee door swing closed. Damn it.

He reached over and grabbed a fistful of synth-leather beside him. The tattooed man jerked out of his grasp, rounded on him. "Fifty bucks," Silas said flatly, cutting him off mid-snarl. "Can you take a punch?"

As soon as the employee door closed behind her, Jessica Leigh hit the hall running. *Shit. Shit. Shit!*

Her hands shook with fear and adrenaline as she pushed into the changing room. A missionary. A *witch hunter,* right in front of her. She'd known who he was, *what* he was the second she'd seen that damn tattoo. It had taken everything she had to bluff it out. Wait out her shift. No sudden moves.

No sudden screaming.

She'd never seen a hunter up close before, never smiled into flinty eyes like he wasn't anything special. Tonight she'd done both. For a solid hour, she'd worked under the steel green edge of his blatant scrutiny.

Now she had to go.

"Damn," she hissed as she swung open her locker. The only three women in the back room weren't paying any attention. Mickey was flying high again, and Ramona and the new girl she didn't know yet were too wiped to do more than wave half-heartedly at her.

Jessie smiled brilliantly back, slinging her heavy black backpack over her shoulder. "Night, girls," she called. She forced herself to head casually toward the bathroom. Shift over, time to go home, no big deal.

She wasn't new at this. Just short-term stupid, apparently.

Slipping inside, she locked the stall behind her and kicked into overdrive. She stripped off the black wig and shoved it into her pack with shaking hands. Slow down, she told herself. Fear and adrenaline could lead to mistakes. She couldn't afford to screw up now. Breathe. *Think.*

She had to get out of here.

Regret clutched at her throat as she peeled off her corset and shimmied out of the matching gold shorts. She should have left two weeks ago, and she knew it. She'd gotten lazy. Complacent.

She'd made friends.

Jessie blinked back a sudden sting of tears as she shook out a pair of faded jeans and stepped into them. "Don't be stupid," she said aloud, striving for steady. She'd known better. Decent pay and a few friendly people wouldn't keep her alive.

Running would. It'd keep her one step ahead of the damned witch hunters and three steps ahead of the rest of the world. It was the only way to survive. Off the radar, out of the system.

Exhausted, run ragged. Downright paranoid. And for what? Certainly nothing even resembling peace and quiet.

She pulled on a gray tank top, wriggled into a matte black neoprene jacket and zipped it up to her throat. In the lower edges of New Seattle's civilized levels, she'd fit right in. It was the work of moments to shake out a short, choppy red wig and pull it on.

She scrubbed off every trace of makeup, flushed the damp wipes down the yellowed toilet, and tucked her sky-high shoes into the backpack. Shoving her feet into plain, thick-soled black boots, she checked the plastic watch on her wrist and frowned.

The whole process had taken less than five minutes. She was too damn good at this.

Jessie creaked open the door, checked the hall. When she didn't see anyone there, she stepped out and made short work of disabling the alarm on the emergency exit. Two seconds later, she was in the home stretch.

The alley flickered dimly under the purple and pink neon light flashing overhead. Girls, girls, girls. "Minus one," Jessie murmured, and shut the door quietly behind her. It clicked with a finality that made her chest squeeze.

It really wasn't fair.

But then, she understood that life hadn't been fair since Mother Nature had flipped a gasket and unleashed rampant destruction on most of the planet. Jessie hadn't even been born when the San Andreas Fault had split so far that Seattle had slid right into the crevasse, but that didn't matter to a world full of terrified, struggling people.

Pre-quake, witches had lived on the fringes of a world that didn't care. They didn't have to hide. They weren't always welcomed everywhere, but they weren't stoned to death in the streets, either. Then the world had gone to hell and the Holy Order of St. Dominic had stepped in to lay down order. Spread some so-called morality.

Five decades should have been enough for the worst of the witch hunts to die down. It wasn't; a fact that Jessie acknowledged every damn time she packed up what few belongings she owned. Instead the Church had slipped into bed with the federal government, and suddenly they were best friends over the barbecue of innocent people.

Worse, the radical Mission—once considered a brand of extremist terrorism—had turned into the Order's right hand. Sanctioned killers at the end of a very deadly leash.

These days, life for a witch was injustice and persecution in a very real sense. It was survival in a society desperate to blame something—hell, anything—for the devastation of fifty years ago.

Hadn't Jessie spent her whole life running? Seen her own mother murdered? Didn't she learn anything from the streets that had tried so hard to chew her up and spit her out?

Hadn't she taught her baby brother the very same thing?

Which was why, she reflected grimly as she raised her collar against the rain, she knew better than to stay in one place for as long as she'd wallowed in the Perch. Stupid.

Jessie could have been the next notch on the Mission's docket tonight. When the hunter had looked her in the eye, she'd have sworn she saw her own death there. It had been damned hard to play at calm, not to panic then and there, take off running right over the bar.

She took a deep breath, barely noticing the familiar stink of rotting garbage and the faint tang of the cold rain. So she couldn't work at this particular club anymore. So what? She'd find another. These lower city levels were chock-full of dives like the Perch.

If Lydia Leigh had taught her children anything, it was how to rebuild.

She stepped off the broken stoop as lurid purple light flickered through the dismal drizzle. Each do-over just got harder and harder, but hell, she didn't have much choice. Witch hunters killed witches.

Exclamation point.

Her boots splashed in stagnant puddles, stirred up loose grit and gravel. She barely noticed when a wide shadow detached itself from the mouth of the alley, then hesitated when it stepped into her path. She didn't have time for this.

Pink neon outlined his heavy build, the blaring smear of tattoo ink and the light-catching saturation of beaten synthleather spiked with metal. Big. Grabby, probably. He seemed the type.

She'd dealt with it before. A casual smile, a flirty wink, a breezy reminder of the bouncers right around the corner, and he'd be back inside eyeballing someone else.

"Nice." The burly man spread his arms to block her way. "Way nice. Easiest score I ever made."

Vapors washed over her; alcohol and the spicy afterburn of something less than legal, even in the Perch.

Just her luck.

She shaped her mouth into a sassy smile and made damn sure it reached her eyes. "You're in the wrong spot, honey. All the best girls are—"

"Right here," he drawled, bending until he was all but nose to nose with her. The scent of sweat and beer wafted over her face in a nauseating combination.

She stepped backward before she could stop herself, giving ground she knew was going to cost her.

Never show weakness.

"I'm on a break," she lied smoothly, praying he was too far gone to notice the heavy backpack slung over her shoulders. "You want to see me dance, you'll want to be inside in five minutes."

"Maybe I'll just see you wiggle right here." He took another step forward. Jessie's body tensed, mouth dry.

Shit. She didn't have *time* for this. Any minute, that hunter was going to come sniffing. The back of her neck itched with the certainty.

Neon popped overhead, highlighting the alley around them in vivid purple. It bled through his full brown beard, glittered off his array of facial piercings and toothy smile. It picked out a lot of sweaty, veined muscle.

And the leering jester inked into one thick arm.

I see death and a laughing joker.

Her heartbeat leaped into her throat. "Fuck," she whispered, and jumped when he laughed.

"Not yet, baby," he said, reaching for her. Her vision tunneled in on the biker's stained, shit-eating smile, and without warning, Jessie's patience guttered out.

She felt herself go. Almost like when she tapped into the power that simmered beneath her conscious mind, but this was sharper. Angrier. Focused.

He was every man who'd ever leered at her. Every man who'd ever groped her in the dark confines of every bar she'd worked at. The ones who'd laughed at her and her baby brother on these goddamned merciless streets.

Jessie's body surged into motion before her brain made the call. She stepped into him, into the wild clasp of his arms, and pure satisfaction rippled through her as his smile cracked into surprise. Her fist collided with his smirk and sent him reeling.

His flat features contorted into shock. Rage. "Bitch!"

Adrenaline pushed her forward; she tried to dart past him, choked on her own collar as a meaty hand snagged the back of her jacket and hauled her back into the alley. Slammed her back against the broken, pitted brick, hard enough to force the air from her lungs. Jessie's vision dimmed as she swung again, connected with something metal on his coat, and yelped as her arm went numb from fingers to elbow.

If the joker gets his hands on you, Jessie, that's it. That's the beginning of it all. Don't stop for him.

Her brother's voice, the memory of it, rang sharply in her head. Too damn late.

She tried to jerk away, cried out again as his fist tagged her mouth. Pain exploded inside her skull, lights flashing violet and pink and red as she dropped to her knees.

Blood pooled on her tongue, coppery and warm. Jessie choked on tears of pain, of humiliation and fury, even as she struggled to get off her hands and knees, and hit him again.

And again. And—

"What the *fuck,*" she heard, and a riot of energy roiled around her. For a dazed moment it looked as though her attacker split into two, dancing awkwardly away from her like two halves of a broken mirage. One staggered upright, thick and meaty, the other long and lean as they wrenched apart. With a bellow, the biker swung at the second man who was nothing more than a trim, fast-moving shadow dancing just out of his reach.

Jessie shook her head hard, forced herself to her feet. She stumbled hastily for the alley mouth. *Get out, run like hell.* She couldn't get caught up here, not as long as that hunter was—*Oh, God.*

Her knees buckled violently. She whirled to plaster her back against the wall, grabbed rough brick for support as she stared at the fighters. *Him.* Shocked, she jammed her fingers against her bleeding mouth.

Neon flickered, seared, and she saw tanned skin, black ink, and rough denim as the witch hunter blocked with his left forearm, snarled something, and curved out a wicked right hook.

His body moved like an oiled machine, brutally efficient as he followed up with two jabs to the drunk's nose and an elbow that crunched loudly on impact.

Blood spurted, near black in the neon light.

"Run!" The witch hunter threw it over his shoulder, only to twist awkwardly when the biker stomped hard on his knee. Jessie saw his face go shock-white, heard his agonized grunt of pain.

Fury and fear forced her to move. She caught her backpack in one hand, swung it with all her might. The black canvas bag sailed through the violent neon air, graceful as a brick, and slammed into the side of the biker's head with a dull crack.

He toppled, slowly.

Jessie stared in horror. He didn't move. God. Had she killed him? She had enough problems without adding murder and cops to the list. She panted for breath, unable to suck in enough air to keep spots from mottling the corners of her vision. Was he dead? She didn't know if a thirty-pound bag could kill someone of that size, and she desperately didn't want to check.

She reeled.

Strong fingers curled over her upper arms. "Hey!"

She blinked. Stared into a face carved from something even more unyielding than the brick surrounding them. "Can you walk?" he asked. Demanded.

Jessie's brain flailed. "Is he—?"

"Try," he ordered, and hauled her bodily out of the alley.

He was limping. It was the only rational thought she managed to form, and wordlessly she ducked under his arm and slipped it over her shoulders. He hesitated, resisting her, but she dug her fingers in to his side and held on. She felt the flex and slide of hard muscle as she fisted her hand in his shirt.

As much as Jessie wanted to slip away from him, use his injury to put as much space between them as she could, she couldn't just leave him there. He'd helped her. She had to help him.

And the truth was, she needed something to hang on to, just for a moment.

She followed his lead as he pointed to a rusty orange pickup truck. He wrenched open the door, half lifted, half shoved her inside the driver's side, and pushed her farther over as he swung up painfully behind her. He wasted no words, and she had plenty of time to study the implacable set of his features as he gunned the engine and slammed it into drive.

Talk about a rock and a hard place.

A witch hunter. And a hero, at least for the five seconds it was taking her brain to process and reboot.

He'd saved her.

She'd saved him, too. She wondered if he'd have been so heroic if he knew who and what she was. She'd bet her tip money that he'd have left her there to die if he'd had any real clue she was a witch.

As the truck pulled a U-turn, tires squealing, Jessie twisted to see if the drunk had moved. She glimpsed him facedown, dead still, exactly where they'd left him. And her bag. Shit!

The hunter took a left, swerved around a trailer. "He'll live."

"Lucky him," seemed harmless enough. Vacuous enough. Jessie glanced at the witch hunter as he adjusted the rearview mirror with one rough hand. Despite his terrifying vocation, he appealed on some deep level. A rough shadow darkened his angled jaw. It framed a mouth that bowed at the top, which she'd noticed the instant he'd sat down at her bar.

She'd briefly toyed with the idea of leaning over the counter and tasting it. Now she was glad she hadn't. Not even for the extra tip money that flirty act would have netted her.

His hair curled in short waves, dark brown and shaggy, and Jessie couldn't help but admire his easy strength as he'd hauled her down half a city block, even despite his limp.

It was the same strength he'd probably developed strangling innocent people in the night.

She set her jaw.

Anger rolled off him in palpable waves, an aura of fury that she didn't need preternatural senses to recognize. Long, all-too-capable fingers gripped the steering wheel with white-knuckled intensity as he drove with purpose.

Drove where?

Death and the laughing joker. Two different people? Shit. Caleb's prophecies never made *sense.*

Jessie scraped back the fringe of fake red hair with one shaking hand. "Thanks for the help and all." His mouth twisted. "But," she continued lightly, "you can drop me off here."

He didn't reply, didn't slow down. Didn't acknowledge her. She bit her lip, winced when it throbbed in protest.

It had to be a coincidence. She'd never heard of a witch hunter saving a witch just to kill her himself. Unless he was a real freak of nature.

Or didn't recognize her in her disguise.

Short red hair, no makeup, street clothes designed to blend; it was a far cry from the vamped-up brunette bartender he'd met. The alley had been dark. He'd seen a woman in trouble.

Could she stake her life on a witch hunter's good intentions?

Would she be heading to her own death if she did?

No. It was still a risk, and the laughing joker hadn't killed her. That didn't mean she was safe. She'd just toppled the first domino of her baby brother's worst prophecy. Christ. Shit.

She wasn't going to die, damn it.

Jessie casually draped her hand on the armrest, her thumb resting on the door release. The second he slowed down, the moment she saw her chance, she'd be gone.

"Don't even try it."

"Try what?"

"We're going sixty. In half a minute, we'll be on the carousel. You'll be a smear if you jump, and I'm not slowing down."

What was he, psychic? Her temper spiked. "I'll take my chan— Let go of me!" His hard, cold fingers were implacable as he gripped her forearm.

"I didn't haul you out of that bastard's rape fantasy to lose you to asphalt," he said flatly.

Jessie's teeth clicked. "I don't need a hero," she gritted out. "Let me go."

He did, but only so he could put both hands back on the wheel. "Stay fucking put."

Her heartbeat roared in her ears. Her lip throbbed, but the small pain was going to be the least of her problems if the jump out of a moving vehicle didn't kill her first.

Steeling herself, she reached again for the latch on the door.

"Your friend was right," he said. "You're a better blond."

